"A woman should have a proper kiss after she gives birth to a son, don't you think?"

Katherine studied Lonnie's rugged features as if she wanted to remember them always.

"I think you're right," he whispered.

She smiled as he touched his lips to hers. The taste of him was rich, tempting and oh, so delicious. She wanted to feel his closeness, his strength, breathe in the unique scent of his hair and skin.

"I think it's time I should be thanking you," she said.

His brows lifted and the corners of his lips turned up with amusement. "I've never been thanked for a kiss before."

Her expression was suddenly serious. "I'm not talking about the kiss. I want to thank you for delivering my baby. I believe you saved both our lives." There was a soft glow in her eyes. "I couldn't have done it without you."

Dear Reader,

Well, the wait is over—*New York Times* bestselling author Diana Palmer is back, and Special Edition has got her! In *Carrera's Bride*, another in Ms. Palmer's enormously popular LONG, TALL TEXANS miniseries, an innocent Jacobsville girl on a tropical getaway finds herself in need of protection—and gets it from an infamous casino owner who is not all that he appears! I think you'll find this one was well worth the wait....

We're drawing near the end of our in-series continuity THE PARKS EMPIRE. This month's entry is *The Marriage Act* by Elissa Ambrose, in which a shy secretary learns that her one night of sleeping with the enemy has led to unexpected consequences. Next up is *The Sheik & the Princess Bride* by Susan Mallery, in which a woman hired to teach a prince how to fly finds herself *his* student, as well, as he gives her lessons...in love! In *A Baby on the Ranch*, part of Stella Bagwell's popular MEN OF THE WEST miniseries, a single mother-to-be finds her long-lost family—and, just possibly, the love of her life. And a single man in the market for household help finds himself about to take on the role of husband—and father of four—in Penny Richards's *Wanted: One Father*. Oh, and speaking of single parents—a lonely widow with a troubled adolescent son finds the solution to both her problems in her late husband's law-enforcement partner, in *The Way to a Woman's Heart* by Carol Voss.

So enjoy, and come back next month for six wonderful selections from Silhouette Special Edition.

Happy Thanksgiving!

Gail Chasan
Senior Editor

Please address questions and book requests to:
Silhouette Reader Service
U.S.: 3010 Walden Ave., P.O. Box 1325, Buffalo, NY 14269
Canadian: P.O. Box 609, Fort Erie, Ont. L2A 5X3

A Baby
on the Ranch
STELLA BAGWELL

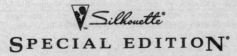

SPECIAL EDITION®

Published by Silhouette Books

America's Publisher of Contemporary Romance

To Marie Ferrarella and Crystal Green,
the two best buddies a writer could have.
Love ya!

SILHOUETTE BOOKS

ISBN 0-373-24648-X

A BABY ON THE RANCH

Copyright © 2004 by Stella Bagwell

This edition published by arrangement with Harlequin Books S.A.

® and TM are trademarks of Harlequin Books S.A., used under license. Trademarks indicated with ® are registered in the United States Patent and Trademark Office, the Canadian Trade Marks Office and in other countries.

Visit Silhouette Books at www.eHarlequin.com

Printed in U.S.A.

Books by Stella Bagwell

STELLA BAGWELL

sold her first book to Silhouette in November 1985. More than fifty novels later, she still loves her job and says she isn't completely content unless she's writing. Recently, she and her husband of thirty years moved from the hills of Oklahoma to Seadrift, Texas, a sleepy little fishing town located on the coastal bend. Stella says the water, the tropical climate and the seabirds make it a lovely place to let her imagination soar and to put the stories in her head down on paper.

She and her husband have one son, Jason, who lives and teaches high school math in nearby Port Lavaca.

My dearest Mary Katherine,

I'm not sure if you will ever see this letter or if I'll even be around to give it to you once you're old enough to read my words and understand what I'm trying to tell you. Although you aren't here with me on the T Bar K, I want you to know that you are my daughter. Your father was a man I loved very much and who loved me in return. Unfortunately, it wasn't meant for us to be together as a man and wife.

To keep our relationship a secret, my generous sister, Celia, has taken you in as her own daughter. But someday I want you to know the truth of your birth and to know your brothers and sister. Leaving you with Celia has left a hole in my soul, and until we can be together, my heart aches to hold you in my arms and kiss your sweet cheek.

Your mother,

Amelia Ketchum

Chapter One

He'd been searching for the woman for three months. To a dedicated lawman like Lonnie Corteen, that wasn't a long time, but in this case, he wasn't working in the capacity of sheriff of Deaf Smith County, Texas. He was working for a friend. And that fact had made it impossible to turn back from this trail he'd been following.

Drawing in a deep, bracing breath, he lifted a black cowboy hat from his head and ran a big hand through dark-auburn hair. There wasn't any use in putting it off any longer, he argued with himself. He needed to get this job done and over with. It had interrupted his life, and his work, for too long. Not to mention his peace of mind.

Climbing the steps to the modest, second-floor apartment, he walked down the covered landing until he found a door with the number 36. There was no doorbell to push, so he gave the door a quick rap with his knuckles. As he waited for a response, he glanced over his left shoulder to the stark parking lot below.

Fort Worth was cold. A strong wind from the north was picking up, making him and the few pedestrians on the streets hunch down in their coats. He'd be glad to get this all over with and get back to Hereford, he thought. Not that it was any warmer there. But West Texas weather in late fall could be extreme. He didn't want to get stranded in this city while a blue norther iced it over. But the uncomfortable weather was only part of the reason why he was eager to get back home. His chief deputy was taking care of things there, but Lonnie wasn't one to leave the security of his county in someone else's hands for any longer than necessary. And this mission he was on here in Fort Worth didn't sit well in his craw. Not at all.

The sound of the rattling doorknob caused him to pull his head back around. He watched as the door opened as far as the security chain would allow and a feminine eye peeped out at him.

"Yes?"

There was a wary note in her one-word question, and since Lonnie wasn't dressed in a uniform or wearing a badge, he pulled out his identification and held it close enough to the opening for her to examine.

"I'm Lonnie Corteen, ma'am. I'm the sheriff of Deaf Smith County, Texas."

Several long moments passed before she finally reached up and pulled back the security chain. When she did, Lonnie found himself looking at a woman in her midtwenties, dressed in a red sweater and a pair of black jeans. Her feet were bare, and her toenails were painted the same bright red as her sweater. But none of those things really caught his complete attention. It was the rounded mound of her midsection that whammed him with surprise.

The woman was pregnant! He'd not counted on this development. Not by a long shot. From all the information he'd gathered, he'd believed she was a single woman, living alone.

"Hello," she said. "Is there something I can do for you?"

Her voice was low, husky and guarded. The last part didn't surprise him. Most people didn't react joyfully when a lawman showed up at their door.

"I'm not sure," Lonnie said and flashed her a brief, reassuring smile. "Are you Miss Mary Katherine McBride?"

She silently nodded and Lonnie could only think how much she looked like Victoria Ketchum. This woman had the same long, dark wavy hair, the same green eyes and elegantly shaped features as his friend back in Aztec.

"That's good. That's real good." Shifting his weight from one boot to the other, he pulled off his hat and held it against his broad chest. "Uh, if I could come in for a few minutes, I need to talk to you."

Shock shot her brows straight up to form slender black arcs above her eyes. Her hand fluttered near her breasts. "Me? You want to talk to me?"

It wasn't good for a pregnant woman to receive a shock, Lonnie suddenly realized. But what the heck was he supposed to do now? He was already here at the door. He couldn't just say oops, he'd made a mistake and leave her hanging with all kinds of questions and worries.

"Yes. If you have a moment."

A moment! Hell, Lonnie, what you need to relay to this woman can't be done in a few minutes. You've got to do this gently, kindly. The girl deserved that much.

Confusion clouded her eyes and furrowed her forehead. As Lonnie studied her perplexed expression, he couldn't help but notice her skin was milky-white and as smooth as the petal of a rose. Not that he went around noticing such things about women. He rarely allowed himself a second look at the opposite sex. But something about this one was causing him to stare.

"I...I suppose I do," she said haltingly. "But—"

Sensing her reluctance, he added, "I'll try to make it as short as possible, Miss McBride."

She pressed several fingertips to her brow. "But I don't understand. Has something happened to someone I know?"

He smiled briefly. "Now, that would be hard to say, seeing as I don't know your acquaintances, ma'am. But I can tell you that this visit is...personal."

"Personal?" she repeated, as though she'd never heard the word before.

Lonnie couldn't blame her for being confused or suspicious. But frankly, he didn't know how to put her at ease without jumping into this thing with both feet.

"That's right." He motioned past her shoulder to the interior of the apartment. "It's as cold as heck standing here on this concrete. May I come in and tell you about it?"

Her eyes traveled up and down the length of him, and

Lonnie felt himself blushing under her direct scrutiny. He'd had women look at him up close before. After all, he was thirty years old and he wasn't exactly homely. But there was something about the way this woman was looking that gave him a mighty uncomfortable urge to squirm in his boots. Especially when he had the strongest urge to keep looking back.

"I suppose," she said in a voice that clearly conveyed she wasn't happy about any of this.

"Thank you, Miss McBride. I'll try not to take up too much of your time."

She stepped to one side and gestured for him to enter the apartment. He moved past her and into a small living room/dining area. A teakettle was whistling shrilly from the direction of the kitchen, and in one corner of the living room a small television was tuned to a twenty-four-hour news channel. Two cats, a yellow tabby and a solid black were curled up together on one end of the couch. The animals seemed not to notice Lonnie's presence, but then maybe they were used to men coming and going in Mary Katherine's apartment.

The idea was an awful one, and Lonnie quickly dismissed it. Even though her midsection was mounded with child, she didn't look the promiscuous sort, and thinking of her in that way bothered him. Apparently she'd been close to some man, though. But that wasn't any of Lonnie's business. None of his business at all.

"I was just about to make some instant coffee, Mr. Corteen. Would you like a cup?"

She tossed the offer to him as she hurried past him and toward the kitchen. He followed slowly as he tried to think of a sensible way to say what he had to say and get out. But there wasn't anything sensible about any of it, and now that he'd discovered she was pregnant that complicated things even more.

Standing at the edge of the tiny kitchen, he watched as she pulled the teakettle from the gas flame and poured it into a nearby cup. He hated instant coffee with a passion. He liked his boiled, the old-fashioned way, so he could taste the grit of the grounds and feel the kick of the caffeine.

"Sounds nice," he lied. "This weather chills me to the bone."

The tiny room was equipped with a full-size cook stove and refrigerator, but the counter space was small and most of that was scattered with dirty dishes, Lonnie noticed. Apparently, Miss McBride wasn't keen on housework or she was short on time.

"We haven't had much cold weather yet this fall, but I hear we're supposed to have snow in a day or two." She pulled down another cup from the cabinet in front of her and filled it with hot water and a hefty spoonful of instant decaffeinated coffee. "Where do you live? Did you say Deaf Smith County?"

He said, "Yeah. Hereford. As I understand it, you used to live in that area, at Canyon."

She turned away from the cabinet counter and looked at him with surprise. "How did you know?"

"I've been trying to find you for three months. I tracked you all the way from Hereford to here."

Clearly disturbed by this announcement, she turned back to the counter and reached for a paper towel. Lonnie noticed she fumbled the piece of paper several times as she sopped up the puddles of water that she'd spilled.

"Well, perhaps we should take our coffee to the living room," she suggested. "It will be more comfortable to talk there."

He nodded in agreement, and she gestured for him to help himself to one of the cups.

"I have sugar or cream if you want," she offered.

Lonnie picked up the cup closest to him. "No, thanks. I like it plain. It's better that way."

She didn't make any sort of reply, and he followed her back into the living room area. As he walked a few steps behind her, she said, "Please, have a seat, Mr. Corteen."

Standing in the middle of the room, Lonnie looked at the couch and the cats. The cats looked back at him. After a moment's indecision, he headed in the direction of a small armchair filled with what looked to him to be a stack of textbooks.

Seeing his intention, Mary Katherine hurriedly stepped in front of him. "Here, let me get those out of your way," she said as she gathered up the books in her arms. "I'm sorry about the mess. I've just gotten off work and haven't had time to do much cleaning."

"There's no need to apologize, Miss McBride. I didn't exactly warn you that I was coming." He'd thought about calling first, but had quickly dismissed the idea. He hadn't wanted to give her the chance to put him off.

While she stacked the textbooks on a nearby end table, Lonnie eased down in the armchair. As he tried to make himself comfortable, she went over to the couch and took a seat next to the cats. The yellow tabby immediately got to his feet, stretched, then climbed onto Mary Katherine's lap.

"Okay, Mr. Corteen, now that we're both sitting, please tell me what this is all about. I can't imagine how you tracked me all the way from Canyon. I haven't lived there in a long time. And it's been even longer since I lived in Hereford."

"Yes. I know." He propped his ankle on one knee and hung his hat on the toe of his boot. "You moved from Canyon about seven years ago to here in Fort Worth."

She looked at him and he could see the wheels in her head spinning at a high rate of speed.

"Why were you trying to find me? Why are you here?" she asked bluntly.

He let out a heavy breath and decided there wasn't any more time for hemming and hawing. "I have some news for you."

She continued to look at him, her eyes wide and waiting.

Lonnie tried again. "Did you ever know your father, Miss McBride?"

Her slender fingers settled on the cat's head and gently stroked him between the ears. "First of all, no one calls me Miss McBride. It's Katherine. And secondly, what does my father have to do with this?"

"Would you please just answer my question? It's important."

She shrugged, and from the dry twist to her lips, she didn't seem to think it important at all. "No. I don't know anything about my father. Except that he was a drifter. He was in my mother's life for a little while and then he was gone."

"What was his name?"

"Ben."

"Ben what?"

Once again her shoulders lifted and fell. "I don't know. Ben was all she ever told me. She didn't want me to know his name—that way I wouldn't think about it and wish that it were mine." Her lips twisted mockingly. "Not that I ever would wish such a thing."

"So you never knew your father?"

Shaking her head she said, "No. He left long before I was ever born and that was that. Mom never heard from him again." Her features wrinkled in wry contemplation. "Actually, I don't think she wanted to hear from him again. She never said much about their relationship, so I always assumed they'd parted on bad terms."

Heaven help him, Lonnie prayed. How was he going to tell this woman that everything she'd ever thought about herself and her parents was all a facade?

Katherine shook her hair, and the long strands fell on her shoulder and down over one pert breast. Lonnie had never thought of a pregnant woman as being sexy, but Katherine McBride had an earthy quality about her that stirred every masculine particle inside of him. The notion embarrassed him and he tried to look at the walls, the floor, anywhere but at her.

"What's this all about, Sheriff?" she asked. "Have you found my father? Is he trying to find me or something?"

"Call me Lonnie," he suggested. "And as for your father—no, I didn't find him. But—" He swallowed and curbed the urge to sigh. "Tell me, Katherine, did you ever know a man called Noah Rider?"

Recognition flashed in her eyes and she smiled. It was the first smile he'd seen on her face since he'd knocked on her door, and the sight made him feel a hundred times worse.

"Yes. Noah was a friend of my mom's. He'd stop by and visit us from time to time. Especially when I was little. I haven't seen him in a long time, though."

Lonnie had been a lawman since he was twenty years old, and during those ten years, he'd been the bearer of bad news on more than one occasion. It was never an easy job, but there was something about Katherine's tender face that made all the right words stick in his throat like wads of dry bread.

"Well, I'm afraid I have bad news, Katherine. I don't know any other way to tell you but…Noah Rider was murdered several months ago—almost a year, actually."

"Murdered!" She stared at him, totally stunned. "But how? Why would someone have murdered him?"

The cat in her lap must have sensed that she was agitated. He slunk off her legs and jumped to the floor.

"That's what I need to explain," Lonnie told her. "And the whole thing is complicated."

Frowning, she made a faint gesture toward the kitchen. "Maybe I'd better go find a cracker or something. My stomach is a little queasy."

"Yeah. Maybe you'd better," Lonnie said quickly, while thinking he'd already made the woman sick. Damn Seth Ketchum! The Texas Ranger should be here doing this himself. It would've made much more sense for him to deal with Katherine McBride. After all, Seth and his family were the ones who'd been trying to find her. Lonnie had only volunteered to do the tracking out of gratitude for an old friend. But somehow Seth had cajoled Lonnie into being the messenger, too.

Katherine started to push herself to her feet and, seeing her struggle, Lonnie immediately jumped up and reached for her hand. "Let me help you," he offered.

Something flickered in her eyes, and Lonnie got the feeling she wasn't accustomed to a man offering her any sort of help, even something as simple as assisting her to her feet. Damn it, where was the father of her baby? He desperately wanted to ask her, but there was already so much to say to her and he didn't have the time or the right to dig into the romantic side of her life.

Not that Lonnie had any personal interest, he assured himself. No, he'd tried a walk down lover's lane years ago and that one attempt had scalded him with pain and humiliation. Since then, romance had been something Lonnie Corteen carefully steered clear of. But it would be comforting to know that Katherine and the baby were going to have support from someone.

"Thank you," she murmured and placed her soft, slender hand in his big palm.

He tugged her gently to her feet and smiled to himself as he watched a tinge of pink fill her cheeks.

"When is your baby due?" he asked.

"In three weeks. And let me tell you, he's really beginning to feel heavy." She pulled her hand from his and carefully put a small space between them.

"He? You already know it's a boy?"

She unconsciously placed a hand over her rounded stomach. "Not exactly. The ultrasound was inconclusive. But I call him a boy anyway. I just have that feeling, you know."

He absently stroked his chin as he continued to study her. "Uh, what about the father? What does he think?"

Damn it all, thought Lonnie, there he went again. He wasn't going to get into this. Her personal life had nothing to do with him. The only thing he needed to be thinking about was getting the message delivered and getting back on the road to Hereford.

With a tight grimace on her face, she turned and headed for the kitchen. "I'll go get that cracker," she said flatly.

Thoughtfully, Lonnie followed and leaned a shoulder against the doorjamb of the opening leading into the small work space. "Sorry," he said. "I didn't mean to get so personal."

She didn't respond to his apology immediately and Lonnie wondered how he could continue with this task if she was angry with him. Suddenly one of her shoulders lifted and fell, and she said, "It doesn't matter. It's no secret that the baby's father skipped out on me."

"Skipped out?"

Her lips flattened to a grim line as she glanced over her shoulder at him. "Yeah. He ran from the responsibility like a scalded cat. But I'm glad now. He would have made a sorry husband and father. Obviously."

She was alone. Her declaration should have made him sad, even mad. Yet all he could feel rushing through his body was unexplainable relief. The emotion took him by complete surprise, and he tried to push the crazy feeling aside as he asked, "Is that what you thought was going to happen? That the guy was going to marry you?"

Looking away from him, she opened the cabinet and pulled down a box of vanilla wafers and a package of Oreo cookies. "Don't all of us girls?" she asked wearily. "I made a bad judgment call. But I'll not make the same mistake again."

Lonnie noticed she didn't sound bitter, more like resolute. And maybe that was a good thing. It was bad enough that this beautiful woman had already been taken advantage of one time. Twice would be obscene.

He didn't make any sort of reply. Mainly because she didn't seem to want or expect one, so he simply watched her fill a paper plate with the cookies.

"Would you care for some?" she asked.

Lonnie started to decline but decided it would be friendlier to accept her offer. And anyway, he hadn't had a bite of dessert after the hastily gobbled burger he'd had for supper.

"Sure. I'm a sucker for sweets. Especially two-crust pies. You ever make those, Miss Katherine?"

She fetched another paper plate from the cabinet and placed it next to the cookies. "Sometimes. Whenever I have the time and a reason." She gestured to the plate. "I'll let you help yourself," she added.

He started toward the cabinet, and she backed up and out of his way. Lonnie was a big, gangly man with long arms and legs and feet to match. He wondered if his size intimidated her or if she was put off by the idea that he was a lawman. Or maybe it was merely the fact that he was a man that made her keep a wary eye on him. In any case, he didn't like the idea of her being skittish around him. He wanted her to trust him. In every way.

Lonnie tossed several of the Oreo cookies onto the

plate, then added a few of the vanilla wafers for good measure. Behind him Katherine said, "A sheriff doesn't come to a person's house just to let him know someone has died. He has deputies for that kind of thing. What are you really doing here?"

Her quickness shouldn't surprise him. She was half Ketchum, he reminded himself, and they were a damn smart bunch. This woman was no more gullible than her siblings.

"Let's go sit down and I'll tell you," he said soberly.

For long moments her green eyes studied his somber face, and then finally she nodded and quickly swished past him.

Back in the living room they both took up the same seats they'd had earlier. After Lonnie had resettled himself, he took a long drink of the coffee and looked across the room at her. She wasn't what most people would describe as petite, yet to Lonnie she seemed small and vulnerable and he wished he could simply rise to his feet and say his goodbyes. He wanted to tell Seth to leave this girl alone. She'd already had enough upheaval in her life. But she *deserved* to know the truth about her parentage, he argued with himself. She deserved to have a family.

"You remember that a few minutes ago I asked you about your father? Well, I had a reason for that," he said. "I wanted to know just what your...what Celia had told you about him."

A puzzled frown puckered her forehead. "I don't understand. I've already told you what little I know about my father."

He let out a long breath and leaned forward in his

chair. "I realize that. But I just don't know how else to get into this, except—" He stopped, shook his head and wiped a hand over his wavy hair. "Let me start again, Katherine, and hopefully I can make some sense to you. I have a friend who's a Texas Ranger. He contacted me three months ago and asked me for help in finding you."

He watched her go very still.

"A Texas Ranger?" she asked.

Her voice was quiet and quavery, and everything inside of Lonnie wanted to go to her and hold her hand tightly between his. He wanted to assure her that she was never going to be alone again. But he was a sheriff and he'd never met this woman before. He couldn't let himself behave in a familiar way with her. It wouldn't be professional. But then, the strange feelings he got whenever he looked at her weren't exactly professional, either. They were a little unsettling.

"Yes. His name is Seth Ketchum. He lives in San Antonio. The rest of his family lives in New Mexico. Does the name mean anything to you?"

Lonnie watched her mull the name over in her mind.

"I don't know," she answered honestly. "It sounds familiar. But Mom never said much about her family or friends. I accused her once of not having any, and she got so angry I never asked her anything else about them."

"So she never mentioned her family? Or a woman named Amelia?"

Frowning, Katherine struggled to remember. "Except for a few cousins out in Arizona, she said her family was gone. As for a woman named Amelia, I remember she used to correspond with someone of that name. She told me that this woman was an old school friend. But, as well as I can remember, I never met her."

"Well, Katherine, I don't know how else to tell you but…there's been evidence uncovered that leads me, and the Ketchum family, to believe that Celia wasn't actually your mother."

She gripped the coffee cup and scooted to the edge of her chair. "Whh…at?" she stuttered.

"It's true," he said starkly. "Celia McBride wasn't your mother. She was actually your aunt."

One slender hand fluttered up to her cheek where the blood was quickly draining away to leave her skin a pasty-white color. Lonnie was so alarmed by her reaction that he left his chair and hurried over to the couch.

Quickly reaching for the cup in her hand, he commanded, "Here. Let me take that before you drop it." After placing the coffee on the floor, out of the way, he squatted on his heels and reached for her hand. "Are you okay? You're not going to faint, are you?"

Katherine closed her eyes and breathed deeply. It was hard for her to tell what was more unsettling—what he'd just told her about her mother, or the fact that he was holding her hand in a very intimate way.

"I…I'm all right," she insisted. "I just—this is all too unbelievable. You're going to have to show me some proof. Good proof." She opened her eyes and looked at him. "I simply can't take your word about this."

"I understand that," he said softly. "And I understand this has given you a shock."

She stared at him, utterly dumbfounded. "A shock! That's putting it mildly. You're talking about my mother!"

He patted the back of her hand while thinking none of this could be good for the baby. Dear God, Lonnie prayed desperately, if he didn't get her calmed down, it might even send her into labor!

"I can see why this whole thing sounds like a wild, made-up story to you. And I don't blame you for not believing it. But I do have a bit of proof. Seth sent a letter with me. One that your real mother received from Celia. Would you recognize your au—well, Celia's handwriting?"

His announcement appeared to frighten her and she drew back in her chair and stared at him with wide, dark eyes. "A letter?"

Lonnie nodded and reached to the back pocket on his jeans. "Yes. I have it right here—"

Grabbing his forearm, she blurted, "No! I don't want to read a letter now!"

He looked at her with confusion, and she blushed profusely and said, "I mean—maybe I need to hear more about this whole thing from you first. Maybe then the letter will make more sense." She paused and the corners of her mouth turned downward in a skeptical frown. "But I doubt it," she added.

"All right." He squeezed her hand and peered anxiously at her white face. Her features were pinched, and Lonnie was shocked to find himself wanting to smooth his hand across her brow. He liked women. And he could list a long string of females who were his friends. But once he'd had his heart broken he'd come to the firm resolution that a friend was all he would ever be to the opposite sex. So why was he suddenly feeling so possessive of this one? Just because she was soft and pretty and about to have a baby didn't make her any different. "If you're sure you're okay."

She let out a heavy breath, and then all of a sudden she seemed to realize she was still holding on to his forearm. Slowly she pulled her hand away from him and settled it on her short lap.

"I'm all right," she said quietly. "Please go ahead."

Lonnie probably should have put some space between them and gone back to his chair. But she looked so fragile, and being close to her made him feel a little more assured. Which was a sure sign he wasn't behaving like himself. Normally he went out of his way to make sure he kept a respectable distance from women.

"I think I should start way back at the beginning," Lonnie said. "I don't know how else to explain things."

She nodded and he went on, "You see, Katherine, it's all about the Ketchum family. They own a huge ranch in northern New Mexico close to Aztec. It spreads over more than a hundred thousand acres and they raise cattle and horses. Mostly to sell for breeding prospects."

"Do you know these people? Personally?" she asked.

Lonnie nodded. "Seth, he's the Ranger, he helped me get elected to the sheriff's position I hold now. And I have visited with his siblings. They're fine, quality people."

"It sounds like they're rich," she murmured as though that was equivalent to having royal blood.

Lonnie shrugged. "Oh, they're not what you'd call stinking rich. But they're well off. They don't have to scrape around to pay their bills if that's what you mean."

"I wouldn't know any of those sort of people," she said wryly.

Well, the Ketchums were the only rich people Lonnie rubbed elbows with, but he kept that information to himself.

"The ranch—it's called the T Bar K—was started by Tucker Ketchum and his brother, Rueben. Tucker was married to a woman named Amelia and her maiden name was McBride. They've both been dead for several years now."

Katherine's eyes swept back and forth across his face and he could see that her mind was whirling like a Texas tornado.

"You mean—this Amelia—she was the woman my mother wrote to? And her name was McBride, too?"

Lonnie slowly nodded. "That's right. She was a McBride before she married Tucker. She and Celia were sisters."

Clearly disturbed now, Katherine began to shake her head in disbelief. "But…but my mother never said anything about a sister or her being kin to some rich people in New Mexico. Why wouldn't she have said something? Those people would be my relatives!"

Once again he felt the unaccustomed need to touch her and reassure her, and this time he didn't resist the urge to reach for her hand. He pressed her soft skin between his fingers and watched her expression turn to total bewilderment.

"They're more than just relatives, Katherine," he said gently. "Seth, Ross and Victoria—they're your brothers and sister. Amelia was your real mother. Celia only raised you for her."

"No! No! That can't be!"

Jerking her hand from his, she shoved herself to her

feet and ran across the room to where a window displayed the dusky skyline of Fort Worth. Lonnie hurried after her, and as he took her by the back of the shoulders, he realized she was crying. Not on the outside where he could see her tears, but on the inside where emotional pain was causing her whole body to shake. The notion of her anguish cut him deeply. Because he understood exactly how she was feeling. In his younger years he'd done a lot of crying on the inside, too. Maybe that was why Seth had thought Lonnie would be perfect for this job. He'd probably figured a man without a family could empathize with a woman who believed she was entirely alone in the world.

"It's true, Katherine," he said gently as he stared down at the shiny crown of her dark hair. "Amelia Ketchum was your mother."

For long moments she didn't say anything, and then slowly she turned and tilted her face up to his. "If that's true," she said accusingly, "then why wasn't I raised with my brothers and sister? Why was I sent to Texas?"

Lonnie glanced away from her, drew in a bracing breath and tightened his hold on her shoulders. "Because you—" He forced his eyes to return to hers. "Because Amelia had been having an affair and she didn't want her family to know about her pregnancy."

Katherine's hands instinctively pressed against the mound of baby she was carrying, and Lonnie could see from the torn look on her face that she couldn't imagine any circumstances that would make her separate herself from her child.

"All right," she said, then swallowed convulsively. "If that's the case, then who is my father?"

"I hate to have to tell you this, Katherine. But your father was Noah Rider."

If possible, she went even whiter, and her lips began to move but no sound was coming out.

"No-No-ah?" she finally whispered.

Lonnie started to nod, but he didn't have time. Before he could respond, she wilted like a sunflower, and he caught her just as she fell against his chest.

Chapter Two

"Whoa! Whoa, now, Miss Katherine! Don't you faint on me!"

With his hands gripping her upper arms, Lonnie attempted to steady her. To his relief, she stayed upright, but her neck couldn't seem to hold her head straight, and her gaze was blank.

Cursing under his breath, Lonnie quickly scooped her up in his arms and carried her over to the couch. As he eased her down on an end cushion and propped a pile of throw pillows against her back, she began to protest.

"You can let go of me now. I'm...okay," she said stammered weakly. "I just had a woozy moment. It's passed now."

Reluctant to loosen his hold on her, Lonnie kept his fingers tightly fastened around her arm as he sat down on the cushion next to her. "I think I'd better take you to the emergency room," he said with concern. "Just to make sure you're okay."

She looked at him, and her cheeks flushed pink, a sign that relieved Lonnie. At least her blood was pumping at a regular rate again.

"No! I'm fine, really. My head swam for only a few seconds. And that's not unusual for a pregnant woman. Believe me, if I feel the least bit woozy in the morning, I'll head to my obstetrician."

The Deaf Smith County sheriff looked at her with faint skepticism. "I don't know much about pregnant women. But you've had a shock and—"

"I'm tough," she quickly interjected. "Besides, now that I've had a few moments to collect myself, I'm beginning to think about all you've said. And I might as well tell you—I'm not at all convinced that I should take any of your story at face value. As far as I'm concerned, a letter doesn't prove anything. Anyone could have written it."

She straightened her slumped shoulders and reached up to push several strands of disheveled hair from her face. The movement caused the grip of his fingers on her arm to loosen, and Katherine likened the feeling to a piece of hot iron being pulled away from her skin. She'd been around men before. Even rugged, outdoor types like Sheriff Lonnie Corteen. Yet she couldn't remember one, including the father of her baby, whom she'd reacted to as violently as she had this man. It didn't make sense. He wasn't what she'd call handsome. He was tall and rawboned and his features were more rough than smooth. Hooded blue eyes set over a big nose. Hollow creases bracketed a wide, roughly hewn set of lips. The angle of his jaw and the jut of his chin were strong, even a little arrogant. Everything about him was potently masculine, and it embarrassed her to be reacting to him in such a downright sexual way.

"No," he said slowly. "A letter doesn't necessarily prove anything. After all, it could have been forged. But for what reason? What would anyone gain out of making up a story like this?"

Katherine couldn't think of one thing anyone might gain, and that unsettled her even more. Saying Celia wasn't her mother was like saying the sun didn't rise in the east. "I would know my mother's handwriting," she quickly informed him.

He looked at her regretfully. "Don't you mean your aunt's handwriting?"

Her nostrils flared as she took in the meaning of his question. "Celia McBride *was* my mother. She's the *only* mother I've ever known. And I…I think it's despicable that you've come into my home and questioned the veracity of my family."

"I'm not questioning anything, Miss Katherine. This is the story Seth Ketchum gave to me. And Seth doesn't lie. He's a Texas Ranger."

And that was close to being godly, Katherine thought as her stomach tilted wildly. Honor and truth were a motto the Rangers lived by. But that didn't mean this Seth person was automatically right. He could have gotten his information confused. It was some other woman, not her, that had been born to Amelia Ketchum all those years ago!

"I'm not saying that your friend is lying about any

of this. I'm just thinking that he could have received misinformation."

The sheriff reached for her hand and she allowed his big fingers to wrap around hers. The size of his hand and the rough skin of his palm reminded Katherine that he was a big, tough lawman. Yet she felt a unique tenderness in his touch as his fingers gently squeezed hers.

Shaken by that contradiction, she glanced away from him and swallowed.

Lonnie said softly, "I understand this is a whole heap of information for you to take in at once, Katherine. And if I were in your shoes, I'd probably be protesting a lot louder than you are. I'm not asking you just to take my word for the truth. I realize you need facts. And so do the Ketchums. That's why they asked me to find you. If you're really their half sister, they want to know it. Don't you?"

She slanted a woeful glance at him as fear of the unknown crept over her like a night shadow. "I don't know. I pretty much like things the way they are."

Sighing, he pushed a hand through his hair. Katherine couldn't help but notice it was thick and slightly wavy, the color somewhere between russet and chestnut. For a person with red highlights in his hair, he had darkly tanned skin. From hours spent in the Texas sun, she supposed. That could only mean he did much more than sit in a sheriff's office behind a wide desk and bark orders to his deputy.

Why are you even noticing these things, Katherine? It isn't like you to be thinking about a man in this way. Stop it! Before it gets you in trouble.

The little voice in her head made her want to laugh

with self-mockery. What was she thinking? A man had already gotten her into trouble. She was facing the future of raising a child alone. But she was bound and determined to do it and do it well. Just as her mother had raised Katherine all on her own.

"But you might like things better with a family," he reasoned.

The suggestion caused a fissure of pain to creep slowly between her breasts. Of course she would like a family. Since she was old enough to remember, she'd longed for siblings. But Celia had always told Katherine that a family had to have a daddy to have babies and they hadn't had a daddy in their little family. As a child, that reason had been enough for Katherine to quit asking her mother to give her a sibling. But later, when she'd grown up, she'd often wondered why her mother had never married and given them a true family. Was it because Celia hadn't really been her mother? No! That couldn't be. The woman simply hadn't trusted men. Ben had hurt her and she'd never wanted to be hurt again. Katherine certainly couldn't blame her mother for being gun-shy about marriage. Especially now that Walt had deserted *her* like a pile of oily rags.

"Maybe," she said to Lonnie. "But being part of a family isn't—it's not just something you can learn how to do! And besides, these people don't know me. And once they did, they might not want me in their family. I don't want to go through that sort of rejection. Not for any reason."

His brows lifted slightly as he studied her face. "Does this mean—are you actually beginning to believe that Amelia Ketchum and Noah Rider are your true parents?"

Was she? No! It was going to take more than a sheriff and a letter to persuade her.

Her mouth set in a grim line, she looked at him. "I'm sorry, but no."

"I'm sorry, too," he murmured as his eyes flicked regretfully over her face. "Because I think you're turning away from a wonderful, loving family."

Her gaze fell to his big brown fingers wrapped around her pale hand. To have such a man as Lonnie Corteen sitting here holding her hand and talking about family was unbearably sweet. So much so that she knew she had to pull away from him. She had to quickly put an end to this whole disturbing episode. Not only the story of the Ketchums, but also her time with this man.

Pulling her hand from his, she slowly pushed herself to her feet. "I understand you're only the messenger and you're trying to help. But I'm really not up to this. In fact, I'm very, very tired. I'm going to have a bite to eat and lie down."

She was asking him to leave and Lonnie certainly couldn't argue. But it bothered him that nothing was settled. It also bothered him to say goodbye to the woman. He felt an unexplainable need to hang around and protect her. From what, he didn't know. Hell, it looked as though he was the only one giving her a problem.

"Yeah. Maybe you should," he agreed. Rising to his feet, he collected his hat from a spot on the floor near the armchair. As he settled it down on his forehead he looked to see she was about to rise to her feet. Swiftly, he waved her back down. "No need for you to get up, Katherine. I'll see myself out. But there is something I need to know before I leave."

Her brows arched with question. "Yes?"

"When can I see you again?"

She sat straight up and stared at him. "What do you mean?"

"I can't leave town with things as they are. We've got to talk about this. You've got to decide what you're going to do so that I can tell the Ketchums."

Katherine said in dismay, "I can't tell you something like that now!"

"What about tomorrow?"

She smacked a palm against her forehead. "No! I don't—I don't even want to think about it tomorrow or the next day! Just go back to Hereford and tell the Ketchums…tell them I'm Celia McBride's daughter and that's all I want to be!"

He was closer to the door than to her, but her words caused him to return to the couch and look down at her. "I can't do that, Miss Katherine. It wouldn't be good for them or for you." He grimaced as he studied her bright cheeks against her pale, pale face. "Do you have a friend you can call? Someone who can come sit with you? You looked pretty peaked, and I don't like the idea of leaving you alone."

Squaring her shoulders, she pressed her lips into a straight line of disapproval. "I don't need anyone. I'm not a weak woman, Mr.— I mean, Sheriff Corteen. Not physically or mentally. I'll be just fine. Don't worry about me."

Lonnie would worry about her, but there wasn't much he could do about her situation. Especially when she didn't want his help. Sighing to himself, he walked over to the door. "All right, I'm leaving. But I'm not leaving Fort Worth. Not until we've hashed this all out."

Lonnie stepped out into the cold night and, across the room, Katherine fell back weakly against the pile of throw pillows.

"I'm telling you, Seth, this isn't going to work," Lonnie said into the phone the next morning as he sat on the edge of his motel bed and swigged weak coffee from a foam cup. "You or Victoria or Ross will have to come here and try to talk some sense into the woman. She doesn't believe a thing I say."

The Texas Ranger on the other end of the phone let out a long sigh. "Look, Lonnie, I'm not a bit surprised the woman doesn't believe the story you told her. My Lord, it sounds crazy even when I hear it myself. Obviously she's going to need some time to let all this sink in."

Lonnie reached for one of the fresh doughnuts he'd collected from the motel lobby. A continental breakfast wasn't like biscuits and gravy, but it would do until he got home.

"Well, that's probably true," Lonnie agreed. "But I sure can't hang around here while it sinks. I've got a county to see after."

"I understand that, Lonnie. If you have to go home, you have to go home. But I was sure hoping you could persuade her to talk to us. She's our sister, we'd like for her to be a part of the family."

Lonnie swallowed a huge bite of the doughnut before he replied. "I tried, Seth. And to tell you the truth, I probably pushed her a little too much. Uh, I haven't told you this part yet. But the woman is expecting a baby. Real soon," he added while recalling the sight of her bulging waistline. "And I felt bad about giving her such a shock. But once I was there, I didn't have much choice."

"A baby!"

"Yep. In about three weeks, she said."

"Is she married?" Seth asked.

Lonnie reached for another doughnut as he tried not to think about Katherine being pregnant and alone. "No. Seems like she doesn't want to be, either. I guess the daddy must have left her bitter about that. Anyway, she appears to be pretty much all by herself. Celia died a couple of years back from kidney failure."

Seth was silent for a few moments, and Lonnie figured his friend was thinking the same thing he'd been thinking since he'd met Katherine McBride last night. She was obviously going to need help. A woman shouldn't bear a child and then come home to an empty house.

"That's not good, Lonnie. Not good at all."

"Well, I could be wrong. She may have plenty of friends who might see after her. I don't know. I tried to ask her about that last night, but she's pretty touchy and more or less put me in my place before I could get anything out of her."

"Hmm. That's a surprise. You always were good with women. That's why I wanted *you* to meet with Katherine. I thought if anyone could talk to her, you could."

Lonnie snorted with disbelief. "Me, good with women? Seth, something must have happened to you since you've gotten married. I've had one...well, one girlfriend in my lifetime, and that was an experience I wish I could forget. Other than helping them cross the street or listening to their civil complaints, I don't know anything about them."

Except that they were unpredictable and capable of dealing a man more pain than any bullet from a criminal's gun, Lonnie thought grimly.

Seth chuckled. "Don't feel badly, Lonnie. None of the rest of us men know about them, either. But you seem to be able to communicate with them. That's why you've got to go back and try to reason with the woman. She needs to go to the ranch where Victoria can keep an eye on her. And since Victoria is expecting a baby herself, it would make it even better if the two women could be close."

Seth's sister, Victoria Ketchum Hastings, was a medical doctor with a busy practice in Aztec. She was also married to the under sheriff of San Juan County, New Mexico, and the two were expecting their second child in January.

"I'm sure Katherine has her own obstetrician. At this late stage of things she probably wouldn't want to leave Fort Worth and change to a different doctor."

"Hmm. See, that's why you're good with women. You think about those little things. I just think about the big picture. Thank God, Corrina understands me. But that still doesn't change the fact that my half sister needs help."

Lonnie swallowed down the last bite of his doughnut before he said, "Well, Seth, I can't tell you how to give her any help. The last thing she said to me was to tell you Ketchums that she's Celia McBride's daughter and that's all she wants to be. I don't think she would welcome any of you into her life. Not now, at least. She needs to simmer on all of this for a while."

"Yeah. But her being pregnant changes things, Lonnie. We don't have time to let her simmer. We need to help her."

Lonnie frowned. "Seth, I don't understand why you feel beholden to help this woman. You've never met her. You don't know what kind of person she is," he pointed out. "She might not be worthy of all this help you want to give her."

"Is that the impression you got from her?" Seth countered.

Heat suffused Lonnie's face. It wouldn't do for Seth to know all the intimate impressions he'd had of beautiful Katherine McBride.

"No," Lonnie agreed with a sigh. "She seems like a nice girl. And it's pretty obvious that she could use a helping hand. But it just surprises me that you and your family have gone to such lengths to find her."

"She's a Ketchum, Lonnie," Seth explained. "Well, technically, she's not, but she has our mother's blood, and that makes her family. Plus, Noah was her father. And we all loved Noah. Maybe we wouldn't have if we'd known he was carrying on a love affair with our mother while he was the T Bar K foreman. But we didn't know it. And anyway, I guess all of us children have agreed that Mom had good reason to look elsewhere for love. God knows, she sure didn't get much from Dad."

He paused, and Lonnie could hear the squeak of a desk chair and then the clunk of Seth's boots against the floor. Apparently his friend was pacing now and that was enough to tell Lonnie how important this whole thing was to the Ketchum family.

"Lonnie, I know you're probably thinking I should let sleeping dogs lie, but I believe Mom would be happy, real happy if she knew we were reaching out to Katherine and attempting to make her a part of the Ketchum clan. That's why I want you to go back there and try one more time. Tell her there's a home waiting for her at the T Bar K. Ross and Bella would welcome her with open arms. We all would."

Lonnie grimaced as he swallowed the last of his coffee. "Hell, Seth, she won't go to your family ranch in New Mexico. The T Bar K is more than seven hundred miles from here. I doubt I could even talk her into going as far as my ranch in Hereford to meet with you, and that's only half that much distance."

There was a long pause before Seth's voice came back in his ear. "That's it, Lonnie! Persuade her to go to your ranch. She can think things over there while you keep a watch on her. Once she decides she's ready to see us, I'll drive up there to meet with her and take her on to the T Bar K."

Lonnie bolted off the bed. He didn't want a woman in his house. Especially a beautiful, pregnant woman! "That's the craziest thing I've ever heard!"

"No. It isn't. Getting her away from Fort Worth is the first big step. Once she's away from her regular routine, she'll begin to think about all this and hopefully—with a little help from you—she'll begin to see the positive side of having a family."

Lonnie groaned loudly. "Hell, Seth, you expect *me* to talk to her about family? That's even crazier. I've never had a family. Not a regular one."

Lonnie's father had been killed in a bar room scuffle down in Agua Prieta when he'd been working in the mines at Douglas, Arizona. Lonnie had only been a small boy of five at the time, but he'd not forgotten his father, a big man who'd come home in the evenings with red dust covering his hair, face and clothes. Gilbert Corteen had been a happy man, who'd often carried Lonnie around on his shoulders and kissed his wife with the exuberance of a man in love.

After his death, Lonnie's mother, Rhoda, had moved Lonnie to Carrizozo, New Mexico, to be close to her aunt. Once there, Rhoda had tried to get over the death of her beloved husband. But not long after they'd gotten settled there, Rhoda's aunt, and her only relative, died unexpectedly of a heart attack. After that, Lonnie could remember his mother walking around in a stupor, hardly ever speaking. One day she'd left him with the neighbors and told him she'd be back shortly to pick him up. But she'd never returned. That had been twenty-five years ago and he'd still never heard from her.

"The Garcias were a family to you," Seth pointed out. "And because you know what it's like to lose your family, you have a common thread between you."

Lonnie wiped a hand across his face and a stubble of whiskers rasped against his fingers. He'd not taken the time to shave this morning. Last night, after he'd left Katherine's apartment, he'd decided he wasn't going to interrupt her life anymore. No matter what he'd told her last night, he didn't intend to stick around and add to her problems. His intention this morning had been to give Seth a quick call, check out of the motel early and head west. But his old friend was doing his best to throw a kink into that plan.

Lonnie could put a stop to the whole thing right now. He could simply tell Seth he wasn't going to see Katherine McBride again. He was going home to Hereford. But he couldn't bring himself to do that. Seth had been too good a friend down through the years. He'd helped Lonnie in more ways than he could count. This was Lonnie's one chance to pay the Texas Ranger back.

"Seth, I told you—she's pregnant. Real pregnant. I doubt she'll agree to any sort of travel."

"Well, you may be right," he said with thoughtful concern. "Just do what you can do, Lonnie. That's all I can ask of you. And be sure to remember how much I appreciate all of this, buddy. My whole family owes you."

"Aw, Seth, don't go making me feel awful. 'Cause we both know I could never repay you for all you've done for me."

"You don't owe me for anything," Seth countered.

No, Lonnie thought, just a job that had given him a measure of prestige and a large enough salary to buy himself a little ranch of his own. Not to mention all the times Seth had helped him behind the scenes on criminal cases. He would be eternally grateful to Seth for all those things.

"So now that we have that out of the way, when are you going to see Katherine again?" Seth went on.

Lonnie rolled his eyes. He couldn't picture himself going back to face Katherine McBride. Not after the adamant farewell she'd given him. Yet just the thought of seeing her again made his heart beat fast. Which was a sure sign something was wrong with him. He didn't let women affect him that way. He'd learned better.

"It will be a miracle if she let's me in the door again. But, all right, I'll go back tonight, after she gets home from work. I'll try to let you know something later."

"Thanks, Lon. While you're trying to persuade Katherine, I'll let the rest of the family know that you've found her."

Lonnie grimaced. "Yeah, well, somehow I get the feeling that finding her was the easy part."

The Tarrant County Courthouse had been Katherine's workplace for the past four years. When she'd first gotten a job as a file clerk in the tax assessor's office, she'd been thrilled. At twenty-one, with a fresh associates degree in business, she'd not expected a cushy job to cross her path. Especially when she had no real connections in Fort Worth to give her that extra push that was often needed to land a good job.

Since that time, her hard work and dedication had gradually inched her upward in the ranks. A little more than six months ago, she'd become the secretary for the tax assessor himself, a job that was hardly ever easy, but one that definitely had much better pay and benefits.

With the increase in salary, her friend Althea, who worked down the hall in tags and licenses, often urged Katherine to move out of her modest little apartment. After all, she could afford something better now. But Katherine wasn't interested in moving to plush living quarters. She was comfortable where she was. And, anyway, she was putting her money in the bank where it would do her the most good once the baby arrived.

As the two women shared a short, afternoon break together in a private snack room situated behind Katherine's office, Althea exclaimed, "That is the most incredible story I've ever heard! Are you sure this man was legitimate?"

Katherine glanced across the small table at the other woman. The tall, curvy, brunette always managed to look sexy in any piece of clothing she put on and, in the process, made Katherine feel like a frumpy, middle-aged librarian. Older than Katherine by two years, Althea was married and the mother of a small daughter. Since Katherine had moved to Fort Worth and found this job, the woman had become her only special friend. Even though she was close to Althea, she'd not set out today to tell her what had occurred last night. But the whole meeting with Sheriff Corteen had simply been too much for Katherine to bear alone and she'd finally ended up relating the whole incident to her friend.

"Well, I didn't call Deaf Smith County to verify that he was the sheriff there, if that's what you mean," Katherine replied.

The sassy brunette raised her brows. "Katherine! Why not? He could have had that ID forged or something!"

Katherine shook her head. "I didn't call because I didn't need to. If you'd met the man, Althea, you'd clearly see that there's nothing phony about him. I'm dead certain he *is* the sheriff there."

"Okay. So he's the sheriff," Althea reluctantly agreed. "But does that mean you believe this story about your parents?"

Katherine shrugged one shoulder as she jabbed a spoon at the ice floating in her tea glass. Their fifteen-minute break was nearly over. She couldn't begin to tell Althea everything that had gone through her mind last night, much less everything she'd felt when Lonnie Corteen had turned her world upside down. Even now, nearly a whole day later, she was dazed and struggling to keep her mind on her work.

"I don't know what to believe, Althea. It sounds— well, it sounds like it's something that might be easily proved. But I'm not so sure I want proof. I'm not so sure I want things to change. You know what I mean?"

Althea looked at her with thoughtful confusion. "Sort of. I think you're trying to say you're afraid to know the truth about your parents because you might not like it."

Katherine nodded slowly. "Yes. That's sort of how I'm feeling. I mean, Celia, my mother, loved me. I have no doubt about that. She was the one who was there to care for me day in and day out. I'm not so sure what I could think about a woman who would give her daughter away. I don't believe I could ever have warm feelings toward her and that would only cause friction with all her other relatives." She stopped and gave her head a sudden shake. "No. I don't think it would be a good thing for me to pursue this."

Althea crinkled up a candy-bar wrapper and tossed it in a nearby wastebasket, then popped the last of the chocolate into her mouth. "Hmm. Well, what about this man—Noah? Suppose he really is your father? Wouldn't you like to know more about him and his family? If I were you, I believe I would."

These were questions Katherine had rolled over and over in her mind last night. But she'd not gotten any answers. Not with that sheriff popping into her head every few minutes, Katherine thought with a measure of self-disgust. She really didn't know what was happening to her. All the extra hormones bombarding her body must be making her act out of character, she decided. She couldn't figure any other reason for the physical reaction she'd felt toward the man. For heaven's sake, she was pregnant! She wasn't supposed to be feeling those sorts of things…was she?

"Katherine? Yoo-hoo. Are you still with me?"

The sound of Althea's voice penetrated her straying thoughts, and she quickly focused back on her friend's face. "Forgive me, Althea. My mind, it's spinning about a mile a minute. And I'm very much afraid that Sheriff Corteen is going to show up at my apartment again this evening. He pretty much implied that I was going to see him again." With a slight shiver, she pushed the tea glass away and shoved her hands through her loose hair. "I don't know what to do, Althea! He says the family wants to see me. And I told him I didn't want anything to do with them. But I have a bad feeling that he isn't going to give up."

Seeing the anguished expression on her friend's face, Althea reached across the table and squeezed Katherine's fingers. "Katherine, honey, you've got to calm down. All this turmoil can't be good for the baby. You've probably run your blood pressure up with all this worrying."

Closing her eyes, Katherine breathed deeply and tried to relax. "I know. You're right. This isn't something that's going to resolve itself in a matter of days. I need time to think."

Leaning forward over the tabletop, Althea looked at her brightly. "Maybe you should take some time off—

go away for a week or so," she suggested. "You have some sick leave coming, don't you?"

"Yes—but I was saving it for when the baby comes. And anyway, work at least keeps my mind—" Pausing, she shook her head. "Who am I kidding? The work I've done today hasn't helped to get anything off my mind. In fact, I think I'd better go back and reproof the letters I typed this morning. They're probably a mess."

Althea gave her a perceptive nod. "That's what I figured. You're not in any shape to be working. Besides, it's almost time for your maternity leave. Why don't you tell Richard that you need to start it early? You know he wouldn't give you any problem about it. My Lord, the man's crazy about you. He's not about to make things hard for you."

Katherine stared glumly at the tabletop. Having the Tarrant County tax assessor crazy about her was not what she really wanted. Richard Marek was a very nice guy and he'd been a wonderful boss to her, but she'd not once given him any indication that she was interested in him personally. Still, she knew that Althea was right. He did like Katherine, a lot. In fact, he'd asked her out on more than one occasion. A woman who was clearly pregnant with another man's child! She'd declined each time of course, but his interest in her had clearly forced her to be much more guarded around her boss.

"I'm not going to exploit the feelings he has for me, Althea. It wouldn't be right. Especially when I have no interest in him."

Althea rolled her eyes and shook her head. "Katherine, you are so prim that sometimes I wonder how you ever got pregnant! And why aren't you interested in Richard? He's good-looking and nice. He has social prestige, not to mention the fact that he could give you financial security."

Frowning, Katherine looked up at her friend. "You make him sound like the perfect man."

"Well, he's certainly at the top of the list of eligible bachelors around here. And you could have him if you wanted him. Your baby would have a daddy. A real daddy."

Maybe she was crazy, Katherine thought, for not liking Richard more, for not giving him the opportunity to have a lasting relationship with her. But he wasn't the sort of man she wanted to live the rest of her life with.

"I don't want a perfect man, Althea. I don't want money or social prestige or an impressive house. I just want a man to love me. Really love me." A man like Lonnie Corteen, she thought. A big, tough man that made her feel like a woman by just looking at her, a man who would fight to the death to protect her and never ever desert her or their child.

Althea laughed mockingly. "And you think Richard doesn't? You won't know until you give him the chance."

Glancing at her wristwatch, Katherine rose to her feet. "I gave Walt a chance and he let me down—bigtime. I'm not ready to give anybody a chance again. I'm not sure I ever will be," she muttered bitterly.

Clicking her tongue with disapproval, Althea rose from her chair, also. "I'm sorry, honey. We shouldn't have gotten off on that subject. You've got enough on your mind already."

Yeah, like who were her real parents? Amelia Tucker and Noah Rider? If that was true, then why had they deserted her? And why did the thought of seeing Lonnie Corteen again make her break out in a nervous sweat?

Chapter Three

That evening Katherine was naked when she heard the knock on the door. With her heart jumping into her throat, she tossed away the towel she'd been drying herself with and reached for a robe lying near the tub. The garment was not exactly what she'd choose for anyone to see her in, much less Lonnie Corteen. The sunny-yellow chenille had long ago faded to the color of dead grass, and in some spots there were clusters of pinholes where the chenille had fallen out. But since she'd just stepped out of the tub and *he* was already at the door, she didn't have much choice.

And it had to be *him,* she thought, as she hastily knotted the belt above the mound of her stomach. Other than Althea, she didn't have visitors. Sometimes annoying sales people knocked on the door, but it was already after dark, and she didn't think a salesman would be out in such cold weather at this time of the evening.

The knock sounded again.

Muttering under her breath, she wiped strands of wet hair from her face. "I'm coming," she called out. "Just hold on!"

Her hurried exertion to get to the door caused her breath to quicken and she was sure there were two scarlet circles to stain her cheeks, but the moment she opened the door and spotted Lonnie Corteen on the other side, she felt most of the color in her face drain away.

Even though she'd expected it to be him, she'd still not been prepared for the sight of his tall, massive body filling the doorway or the rugged face smiling back at her.

"Hello, Katherine."

She swallowed and unconsciously pushed at the tangled hair on her shoulders. "Hello," she replied.

He stepped forward and moved from the shadows. Katherine immediately spotted something nestled in the crook of his arm. A step closer to the light and her eyes zeroed in on a bouquet of pink roses wrapped in green cellophane paper.

"Uh, what are those for?" she asked bluntly.

A lazy grin spread over his face. "I was hoping a dozen roses would help you to forgive me."

Dumbfounded, she stared at him. She'd only known this man for a few hours! Walt had dated her for months and she'd never seen flowers from him. Or, for that matter, any man.

"Forgive you? You didn't do anything. You were simply a messenger."

"I upset you last night. Believe me, Katherine, that wasn't my intention."

How could she turn him away from the door now? Not that it had been her intention to send him on his way. But she'd been telling herself all evening that if he showed up, her best recourse would be to send him away. But how could she shut the door on a face like his? Especially when he was holding the most beautiful roses she'd ever seen.

A gust of freezing wind whipped around him and tugged at the lapels of her robe. Clutching the fabric against her throat, she said, "You'd better come in before we both freeze to death."

He quickly stepped inside and she got a faint whiff of aftershave and leather. The scents were as masculine as the man himself, and she realized with a guilty start that, compared to Lonnie Corteen, her baby's father had been more boy than man.

"I hope I'm not disturbing you," he said as he walked to the center of the small room. "Were you getting ready to go out?"

Her, go out? The question was almost laughable. She'd never been a go-out person. Even during her relationship with Walt, the two of them had rarely gone out for dinner or any sort of entertainment. She'd always been a loner and he'd been more than happy to go along with her choice of the quiet life. That is, until he'd learned about the baby. Then he'd not been happy about anything. Especially her.

Carefully locking the door behind her, she turned to him. "No. I...I'm afraid I just got out of the bath. Would you, uh, excuse me while I go get dressed?"

Lonnie was trying to be polite and not stare, but he couldn't quite keep his eyes off her. She was the prettiest thing he'd ever seen in that old yellow robe that clung to her breasts and the baby she was carrying. Her long dark hair was wet and lay in curled ringlets upon her shoulders. A soft pink color washed her cheeks and lips, and her skin gleamed with tiny beads of moisture.

"Sure. Take your time. I'll just make myself comfortable." He glanced down at the roses. "What about these? If you'll tell me where to find a vase, I'll put them in water for you."

He was sure he wasn't the sort of man she would associate with flowers. His big hands were made for collaring criminals, or reining in a high-spirited horse, not clutching the fragile stem of a rose.

She shot him an apologetic look. "I don't have a vase. I did. But I accidentally broke it. I have a big Mason jar in the cabinet where I store the glasses. You might use that," she suggested.

"Fine. That'll be dandy. You go on now and get dressed. I'll take care of these."

Nodding, she turned on her bare feet and hurried out of the room. Lonnie went to the tiny kitchen and found the Mason jar. As he filled it with water and plopped in the roses, he figured he'd made a mistake at the grocery store where he'd picked these up. He should have gotten a poinsettia. Thanksgiving was only a couple of weeks away. The seasonal flower would have been more fitting. But the roses had looked more romantic to him. Not that he had romantic designs on Katherine McBride. No, sir. He wasn't about to let himself get that starry-eyed sickness that turned men into fools. But heck, all women liked roses, didn't they? And he needed her in a soft mood if he was ever going to get her to listen to the Ketchums' side of things.

Who are you kidding, Lonnie? You got her the roses because you wanted to see her face light up. You wanted to do something special just for her.

Ignoring the mocking little voice, Lonnie went to sit on the couch. His hat was resting on his knee and the toe of his boot was tapping the air when Katherine finally returned to the living room wearing a pair of black slacks and a pink turtleneck sweater. Her damp hair was fastened at the nape of her neck with a tortoiseshell clip, but she hadn't bothered to put on any shoes. Her pearly red toenails peeped out at him from beneath the hem of her slacks.

Rising to his feet, he clutched his black felt hat between both hands. "Thank you for agreeing to see me, Katherine. I really wasn't sure you'd let me in."

Katherine's gaze swiveled over to the jar of roses he'd placed in the center of the small wooden dining table. The blossoms were so pretty, like a ray of bright sunshine on a cold, dark day.

Suddenly Katherine felt more awkward than she could ever remember feeling and the baby must have sensed her unease because he was kicking like an acrobat. She smoothed a hand over the rolling movement beneath her belly. "I'm sorry I was so hateful to you last night. That's not normally my nature, Mr. Corteen. I guess—"

"It's not Mr. Corteen," he interrupted.

She pulled her eyes back to his lean face. "Okay. Sheriff."

He stepped forward and she watched his big fingers slowly move the hat round and round between his hands. "It's not Sheriff, either. Call me Lonnie. Everybody else does."

She doubted his subordinates called him Lonnie, but she wasn't going to bring that to his attention. She already felt as if she was getting too personal with this man. Or maybe it was just her thoughts that were getting too personal. Either way, she could hardly keep her eyes off him. His presence was just too strong, too sexy for a woman to ignore.

"Okay, Lonnie. As long as you'll accept my apology."

A slow smile spread across his face, and Katherine felt something inside her begin to melt like butter on a hot biscuit.

"Let's forget all that and start over," he suggested. "Have you eaten supper?"

She shook her head. "Not yet. I haven't had time to get any sort of meal together."

"Then let's go out and eat," he suggested. "My treat. Anything you'd like."

Tilting her head to one side, she took a moment to contemplate his invitation. "Hmm. Flowers and dinner. Sounds like you're trying to charm me. I wonder why."

He let out a casual chuckle, but inside he was wondering if Katherine was right. Was he trying to charm this woman? If he was, then he needed to quit it and fast. He and women didn't mix. Not romantically. They liked him as a friend, not a lover. And there wasn't any reason to think that Katherine would be any different.

"There's no charm about it," Lonnie said. "I'm hungry and I hate to eat alone. We could both sit here and talk with our stomachs growling. But that really wouldn't make much sense, now would it?"

Put like that, it wouldn't make much sense. And it would be nice to eat something other than what she scrounged up in her own little kitchen, she decided.

"Not much," she agreed with a tentative smile. "Just give me a few moments to put on my shoes."

"What about your hair?" he asked, his eyes traveling over the curling tendrils framing her face. "Maybe you should dry it a little before you go out. You wouldn't want to get a cold. Especially in your condition."

Once again her lips parted with surprise. The men she'd known had never been thoughtful about such little things, and it took her aback that this big lawman would consider her welfare in such a nice way.

"Well, I wouldn't want you to have to wait," she said.

He gave her a lopsided smile. "Take your time. While you're gone, I'll see if I can make friends with your cats."

Katherine hurried to the bedroom and pulled on a pair of ankle boots, then rushed to the bathroom and plugged in the hair dryer. With it blowing on high speed, she hastily brushed through her hair, while asking herself what on earth she was doing agreeing to go out with a virtual stranger.

Because he knows things about your family that might be important.

Snorting under her breath at the little voice in her head, she yanked the brush through a mass of tangles.

There was no secret surrounding her family. It was Celia. That's all the family she'd ever had.

Well, he is nice.

So were a lot of other men, she mentally argued. That didn't necessarily make it wise for her to go out to dinner with any of them.

He brought you roses. Roses! No man has ever done that just for you!

Snap out of it, Katherine, she silently commanded. A flower is just a flower. You can buy them on most any street corner. Besides, deep down you know he only brought them to you because he wants something from you. That was the way with all men. And this one was no different.

But for some reason she wanted to think Lonnie Corteen was different. She wanted to think he really was concerned about her emotional and physical well-being. Yeah, she thought dismally, just like she'd wanted to believe that Walt had really loved her.

Of the two cats, the yellow tabby was the most sociable. By the time Katherine had returned to the living room, the animal was purring and rubbing his arched body against Lonnie's leg.

"Where's Sophie?" Katherine asked.

Lonnie glanced up and was instantly surprised at the difference in her appearance. Her hair fell in gentle waves around her face and down onto her shoulders. A dab of pink color glistened on her lips and cheeks to give her skin an even more luminescent glow. She was a darn pretty woman, Lonnie decided. Way too pretty for the likes of him.

"If you mean the black cat," he answered, "she shot

under the couch and hasn't resurfaced. But this one seems to like me."

An indulgent smile twisted Katherine's lips. "Nigel likes most everybody."

Lonnie chuckled under his breath. "I should have known. And here I thought I'd become a special friend." He rose to his feet and looked at her questioningly. "Ready to go?"

"Yes. Just let me get my coat."

She went to a small closet near the front door and pulled out a tan suede coat lined with sheepskin. Before she could shove her arms into the sleeves, Lonnie came up behind her and helped her on with the heavy garment.

The masculine scent of him surrounded her and all sorts of thoughts zinged through her head as his warm fingers inadvertently brushed against her neck.

"It's mighty cold out there," he said softly. "You really should pull up your hood."

"All right," she murmured in agreement.

He adjusted the hood of her coat onto her head and tied the leather laces beneath her chin. She held her breath as his big hands came close to her face.

"There, now," he said with a satisfied grin. "That ought to keep you toasty."

Katherine considered telling him she was a pregnant woman, not a fragile egg that might break at the slightest jar. But she didn't. It was nice—oh, so nice—to be fussed over. She wanted him to know she appreciated his thoughtfulness.

"Thank you, Lonnie."

He gave her a faint smile and reached for the door.

After turning out the overhead light, Katherine followed him onto the landing, and he quickly took her by the arm.

"These steps are dangerous for a woman in your condition. One little misstep and you'd go toppling down. And God only knows what that would do to you."

The strong band of his fingers could be felt even through the thickness of her coat. She felt herself shiver and knew it wasn't from the cold wind whistling across the courtyard.

"I'm very careful. I've lived in this apartment building ever since I came to Fort Worth. So I'm used to the stairs. And the noise," she added jokingly.

He glanced at her. "You like living here? In Fort Worth, I mean."

She shrugged. "It's okay. Sometimes I don't like the bigness of it, but I do have a good job."

"You work in the county appraisal office," he stated.

Her brows lifted in brief surprise and then she seemed to accept that he'd already learned things about her that she'd not expected him to know.

"Yes. I'm secretary to the tax assessor."

Lonnie hadn't known that. Only where and what department of the county courthouse she worked in. The news worried him. Not that any of this should be his concern. But if he'd ever had a chance of persuading her to travel to West Texas with him, it had just sunk to the bottom of the lake. The woman obviously wasn't about to leave a choice job to go off to investigate some wild story about a mother who was already dead anyway.

"That's good. It must be a relief to know you have a secure job. What with the baby coming and all," he reasoned.

They reached the bottom steps, and he kept his hand firmly around her arm as he guided her toward a white, club cab, pickup truck. Katherine allowed him to help her into the passenger seat and then he shut the door and skirted the hood to take his place behind the wheel.

While they both buckled their seat belts and he motored the truck out of the parking lot, Katherine thought about her job and the conversation she'd had with Althea this afternoon. There was no doubt she'd been fortunate to land her secretarial position. And when she'd first taken on the job, she'd been living on a cloud. But little by little she'd felt Richard getting close to her. Closer than he should. Not physically. No, he'd always been the perfect gentleman. Yet he didn't try to hide the fact that he wanted to involve himself with her day-to-day life, and that made it hard to keep a brisk business manner between them. The whole situation made her job awkward and uncomfortable. She didn't want any man in her life now. Period.

"Well," she said in an absent voice. "I don't think there's any perfect job."

He glanced her way, and she frowned at the almost hopeful look on his face.

"You don't like your job?" he questioned.

Frowning deeper, she shook her head. "I didn't say that."

"Oh. I guess I must have mistakenly gotten that impression."

He was too intuitive, Katherine thought. No telling what else the man might be picking up from her. Dear Lord, it would be highly embarrassing if he ever realized she found him physically attractive.

"Look, it's a good job. I'm not getting rich by any means. But it's more money than I've been accustomed to having," she said, her voice just the teeniest bit cross. "I just wish there were a few things different about it, that's all. But like you said, a person's fortunate not to have to worry about their financial security."

The vents in the dash were blowing lukewarm air. She held her cold hands toward one and worked her stiff fingers.

"It's grown even colder since this afternoon," she said. "I hope we're not in for a long spell of this."

"The truck should get warmer in a minute or two." He merged into busy traffic on a four-lane street and reached up to adjust his rearview mirror. "Do you have a special place you like to eat?"

Katherine almost wanted to laugh. She couldn't remember the last time she'd been out to eat. It just wasn't the same when a person dined alone.

"No. You choose," she told him. "I like most anything. Fast food will be fine, if that's what you like."

"I don't like *fast* anything. Especially my food."

She surveyed his profile for a few seconds, then cleared her throat and settled back in her seat. She wasn't about to comment on that remark. Besides, she needed to figure out how she was going to get through this evening without making a fool of herself, and moreover, how she was going to end Sheriff Lonnie Corteen's pursuit.

A few minutes later he parked at a Mexican restaurant, and they were ushered to a small round table in a corner flanked by a plate glass window on one side and a collection of huge tropical plants on the other. In the middle of the table, a fat red candle flickered inside a glass holder.

Lonnie seated her on the side of the table next to the plants, then took the chair directly opposite her. A waiter appeared almost immediately with fresh guacamole, tortilla chips and tall glasses of ice water. Once he left to give them a few moments to study the menu, Katherine looked around her.

The restaurant was old. The floors were bare, scrubbed wood and the Formica tables and chairs were all different colors and dated back to the fifties, at least. Numerous photos adorned the walls, most of them shots of Fort Worth during its early days as a dusty cattle town. From somewhere in the direction of the kitchen, Tex-Mex music was playing quietly on the radio. At the moment the restaurant was quiet, with only a few other couples scattered across the small room. But Katherine wasn't surprised at the lack of diners. The bitter weather was keeping most Texans indoors.

"You already know what you want?" he asked as he noticed her closing the menu and laying it to one side of the table.

She nodded. "Carne Guisada. This is just the weather for it."

He liked the stewed beef she was talking about, but he wasn't in the mood for it tonight. He wanted something hot and spicy that would burn his tongue and keep his mind off the beautiful woman sitting across from him.

Lonnie scooped up a hefty amount of guacamole on

a chip. "I guess I should tell you that I spoke to Seth this morning. He was delighted that I'd managed to locate you. But he was also worried."

Katherine watched him pop the appetizer into his mouth and chew. Like last night, she was once again overwhelmed by the sheer size of his body and the craggy masculinity of his face. As soon as he'd taken his seat, he'd pulled off his black Stetson and placed it under his chair. Now her eyes glided over deep-auburn hair that waved loosely back from his face and curled slightly against his neck. Candlelight flickered amber highlights over the thick strands and along the rough angles and planes of his features.

Her covert study of him sent her mind off on a totally different tangent, and for a few moments she forgot what he'd been saying. Something about the Ranger and his being worried.

Katherine glanced away from him as embarrassed heat flooded her face, and she quickly reached for a chip and scooped it into the guacamole.

"I still don't know why he should be worried about me," she finally said. "I don't have any problems." At least she didn't have, until the sheriff of Deaf Smith County had shown up on her doorstep, she thought.

"You're pregnant."

She looked at him, her ire suddenly rising. "You told him that?"

Lonnie shrugged. "Why not? It's not a secret, is it?"

More hot color swept into her cheeks. "No. But it's none of his business!"

He reached for more chips from the basket in the center of the table. "I beg to differ. The baby is his little niece or nephew. Of course he's concerned. He knows you're single and could use some help."

Katherine sputtered, but was unable to come up with one word before a waiter came to take their order. Once he was gone, however, she said, "Look, Mr. Corteen—"

"Lonnie," he interrupted. "You sure do have a time remembering instructions."

She released a long, impatient breath. "Okay. Lonnie. Just so you understand, I've been taking care of myself for a long time. I don't need anyone to take care of me or my baby. Got it?"

Leaning back in his seat, he bestowed her with an indulgent smile that came across as more sexy than anything. As Katherine looked at him, she wondered how she could have been so stupid as to let herself be lured into spending more time with this man. He was dangerous to her peace of mind. Somehow she'd known that from the very first moment she'd laid eyes on him.

"Boy, you're a touchy little thing, aren't you? I wasn't trying to imply that you can't take care of yourself. It's just that when a woman is in…a delicate condition, I think it's nice and proper for her to have support."

"From a man?" she asked with sarcasm.

His gaze swept up and down the part of her that wasn't covered by the table. "Well, where I come from that's the normal procedure."

She wanted to be indignant. She wanted to point out to him that women of today were independent. They didn't need a man to make them happy or keep them safe. Yet his old-fashioned philosophy touched a spot deep inside her, a place that had always yearned to have a family, a whole family, and to be loved by a special man.

She breathed deeply and cursed as a ball of emotion burned her throat. Damn hormones. They were making her a nutcase. And the man sitting across from her certainly wasn't helping matters.

"Sorry," she mumbled. "I guess I've been sounding like a regular witch of the west. I just don't know what to think about all of this stuff you've been throwing at me. To tell you the truth, I haven't had time to absorb it all."

A slow smile spread across his face. "I can sure understand that, Katherine. It's not a simple story."

She told the tension in her body to relax. This man wasn't going to hurt her. And she didn't have to believe anything he told her, or do anything he might suggest that she do. All she had to do was make him, and herself, believe that she wasn't interested in the Ketchum family.

Their meal arrived and Katherine dug hungrily into the stewed beef and accompanying refried beans and Spanish rice. She'd been trying to hold her weight down to within the guidelines the doctor had given her and so far she'd succeeded. But it was a difficult thing to do when she felt ravenous almost every minute of the day. The notion made her suddenly wonder what Lonnie thought about her appearance. Probably that she looked like a sow just ready to litter, she thought drearily.

Across the table, Lonnie spoke and reined in her wandering thoughts. "You might be interested to know that your sister, Victoria, is a doctor. An M.D. She has a practice in Aztec."

Katherine stiffened. "The woman isn't my sister," she said flatly.

"How can you say that without looking at any of the evidence?"

She grimaced with denial. "I don't want to look at the evidence. Besides, it takes more than blood to make two women sisters."

"Hmm. Well, I suppose I can't argue with you on that. Frankly, I wouldn't know about siblings or what it's like to have a brother or sister."

Curiosity got the best of her. "You never had any?"

He shook his head. "No. My mom was a sickly woman. I think it was a miracle she gave birth to me."

"Are your parents living now?"

Lifting his gaze from his plate, he looked at her. "My dad was killed in a barroom fight. That fact makes it sound like he was a drinker and a brawler. But he really wasn't. He'd simply gone there to pick up some money that a man owed him for handiwork. Instead of giving him the money, the guy pulled a knife on my dad. He was dead before the police could get there to stop it."

Shaken by his story, she said, "Dear God! What about your mother?"

"My mother—I don't know where she is. I haven't seen her since I was about six years old."

Katherine suddenly forgot about Celia and the Ketchums. This man seemed the epitome of someone who'd been raised in a regular, loving family. But apparently his life so far had been anything but regular.

"Why? What happened?"

Lonnie finished chewing a bite of stuffed jalapeño

before he made an effort to answer. And even then he wasn't quite sure what to say. It wasn't often that he talked about his parents. Especially his mother. Thinking of the woman made him uncomfortable, like a festered splinter that didn't actually hurt. Unless you touched it.

Glancing at Katherine, he said, "I can't really say what happened to my mother. I guess she couldn't take losing her husband. Everyone that knew her says she went a little crazy after he died. I was old enough to sort of remember her acting strangely. But then most everyone behaves differently when they lose a spouse, don't they?"

"Of course," she murmured as her heart went out to him.

"Right," he said with a grimace. "So everybody was shocked when she up and disappeared. They all thought she'd simply been grieving."

Katherine frowned. "Disappeared? How do you mean?"

"One day she dropped me off at the neighbor's and said she was going to the grocery store. She never came back to pick me up."

"Maybe she ran into foul play," Katherine suggested. She didn't want to believe a mother, especially this man's mother, could so callously leave her child behind. "Was there an investigation?"

Lonnie nodded. "A lengthy one. It appeared she simply drove off and never came back. They found her closets empty and a few other indications that she'd left of her own accord."

"Oh. That's—well, I can't imagine what that must have been like for you."

His shrug belied the hollow sense of loss he carried around in his heart. "It hurt. That's what it was like. But the family she'd left me with took me in like I was one of their own. I was fortunate in that way." He leveled his gaze at her. "So you see, I don't know much about mothers and fathers or brothers and sisters. Except what it's like not to have any. That's why I know if I was in your shoes, I'd be dancing a jig, breaking my neck to get to my family."

She could understand his thinking. She really could. But to leap toward the unknown was a scary thing. What if she did go to New Mexico, meet the Ketchums and get to like them, get to believe they really were her relatives and then find that the evidence about their mother had been all made up or was merely gossip? She couldn't survive that sort of letdown. Even worse, what if the Ketchums decided they didn't like her and shunned her? Wouldn't that be worse than knowing you had a family in the first place?

Gripping her fork, she leaned forward and looked at him anxiously. "Then what do you think I should do?" she asked.

Her question appeared to catch him off guard, and then he suddenly shot her a broad smile and reached for her hand.

"I'll tell you what you're going to do, Miss Katherine. You're going to go home with me."

Chapter Four

"Go home with you?" Her mouth gaped like a dying fish as she leaned across the table toward him. "Did I hear you say that?"

Lonnie swallowed and wondered why he felt as though he was about to get on old Roaney, one of the meanest, most unpredictable horses he'd ever owned. He'd thrown Lonnie several times over the years, but thankfully Lonnie was still around to talk about it. Having Katherine as a houseguest couldn't be any more dangerous.

"You sure did."

A strange giggle burst past her lips and she slapped her palm over her mouth. "You're kidding. Right?"

His expression sobered and he tightened his hold on her hand. "No. I'm dead serious. I want you to come home with me. To the Rocking C—that's my ranch out near Hereford. A thousand acres of fine grassland," he added proudly. "You'll like it there. It's quiet and far away from any city noise. It'll give you a place to rest and think—about what you want to do."

Dear God, he was serious, Katherine thought wildly. Her heart began to lope at a dizzying speed. "I—there's no way I would go home with you!"

He actually blanched, and Katherine felt oddly ashamed of herself as he slowly, deliberately pulled his hand away from hers.

"Well," he said in a resigned voice. "I expected that from you."

As though the subject was closed, he picked up his fork and began to eat. Katherine stared at his bent head and wondered why she felt awful. She didn't owe this man anything.

"Well, don't take it personally," she said after a few moments passed.

He looked up at her and she inwardly winced at the wry little twist on his lips. "Don't worry, Katherine. You didn't hurt my feelings. I'm pretty much used to women reacting to me like that." The wry expression on his face turned humorous. "Not that I go around asking women to go home with me. This is…different."

Frowning, she shook her head. "Well, any normal, red-blooded girl ought to be flattered by an invitation from you."

His face brightened with a grin. "You think so?"

Katherine felt her cheeks growing hotter by the second. "Sure I do. You're a nice man. I just can't go with you—for other reasons."

Leaning back in his chair, he folded his arms against his broad chest. "Other reasons? Like what?"

In an attempt to appear casual, she picked up her fork and poked at her food. "It should be pretty obvious. I don't know you. Not really. And I have obligations here. Like my job, among other things. Besides, running off with you to Hereford doesn't make a lick of sense."

"You'd be closer to your brother, Seth. The minute you gave him the word, he'd drive up to see you."

With her fork halfway to her mouth, Katherine paused to look at him. "So that's what this is all about. The Texas Ranger put you up to this."

He nodded and she noticed he didn't seem to be the least bit embarrassed by the admission. But then, why would he be? Katherine asked herself. Lonnie hadn't invited her to his ranch because he was attracted to her. He was simply doing it for a friend.

"He doesn't want you to be alone when you have the baby. And frankly, I don't, either."

Too bad Walt hadn't felt that way, Katherine thought dourly. But then it was probably for the best that he'd shown his true colors. It would be even more devastating to marry a man and discover he didn't love you. And now that they'd gone their separate ways and she'd had time to think about it, she wasn't at all certain that she'd loved him. Walt had been a companion and he'd eased her loneliness, but that wasn't the same as love.

"Why should that matter to you?" she asked him.

He shrugged. "Just because I'm a lawman doesn't mean that I'm heartless."

Oh, he wasn't heartless. She'd noticed that about him during the first five minutes she'd met him. He was a big man with a compassion to match. That was one of the reasons she couldn't trust herself to go to the

Rocking C Ranch with him. He would be kind enough to let her lean on him. Both mentally and physically. And she didn't want to use him like that. It wouldn't be fair to either of them.

"I never thought you were. I just meant—well, you don't know me. What happens to me shouldn't matter to you."

She was darn sure right, Lonnie thought. Katherine McBride's life shouldn't mean anything to him. But he was feeling himself being drawn into her problems. He was already starting to imagine her in his house, sleeping in one of his beds.

"I do know you, Katherine. More than you think. I've been trailing you for three months now. I know where you lived as a child. Where you went to elementary school and where you and Celia lived when you moved to Canyon. I know where you went to high school and college, when you went to work in the tax assessor's office and how long you've lived in Fort Worth. I know that you lived with your…aunt until she died at the age of sixty-five from kidney failure and that you took care of her and drove her back and forth to the clinic for dialysis in between your college classes."

Her heart winced as she thought about those terrible days when her mother's health had begun to rapidly fail. Katherine had felt so helpless as she'd watched her only relative slip away from her. Now she had no one. No family to call on or lean on through happy and sad times.

"Don't call Celia my aunt," she muttered. "She was my mother. My only mother!"

"Sorry. I'm not trying to be insulting. I guess I've just

known the truth for a while now and I don't think of Celia McBride in those terms. Not when I know that Amelia and Noah were your parents."

Katherine put down her fork and gazed pointedly at his empty plate. "If you're finished eating, I need to get home."

She was vexed with him because she didn't want to think about the Ketchums, Lonnie thought. She probably believed that once he left Fort Worth, her life would get back to normal and she'd be able to put the whole matter out of her head for good. But it wasn't going to work that way. She would go on thinking and wondering, until one of these days she would feel compelled to know about her real parents.

"Sure. I'll motion to the waiter for the check. Unless you'd like to stay and have dessert."

Katherine shook her head. "I'm full. Besides, it's not good for me to eat rich sweets." Nor sit here and be charmed by a man who could never be a permanent fixture in her life.

Lonnie paid for their meal, then helped her with her coat. Once they were out of the restaurant and in his truck, Katherine was embarrassed to think she was behaving like a petulant child. Especially when this man had been nothing but kind to her. After all, it wasn't his fault that her parentage had come into doubt. He'd simply been a courier.

"I'm sorry I caused you to cut your meal short," she said as he pulled onto the thoroughfare. "I guess I'm just an irritable pregnant woman."

He glanced her way. "Forget it. I'd already finished everything on my plate. You're the one who didn't eat."

A sigh slipped past her lips. "I had plenty," she said in an absent voice, then her head turned earnestly toward him. "You were serious a few minutes ago, weren't you? When you asked me to go to your ranch."

He nodded. "I was serious."

For some reason she felt cornered, which didn't make sense. This man wasn't pressuring her in any way.

She breathed deeply. "Well, surely you know that wouldn't make sense. I have a job here. My life is here. Why would I want to go to West Texas with you?"

"Could be it would do you good to get away from the everyday grind for a while. Especially since the baby will be here soon."

He was right about that. It would be heaven to be able to rest and relax, to not have to deal with Richard hovering over her. But living with a sexy, single sheriff wasn't the way to go about getting relief.

"That's another thing," she said. "I doubt my obstetrician would allow me to travel. Not that I'm considering going."

He didn't make any sort of reply and after that they both remained silent until he pulled into the parking lot of her apartment building.

"Lonnie, thank you—"

"Katherine, I really—"

They both stopped abruptly as their words tangled together and then Katherine smiled briefly and gestured for him to speak first.

He parked near the staircase leading up to her apartment but left the engine running so that the heater would keep them warm.

Turning slightly toward her, Lonnie caught her gaze in the semidarkness. "I was just going to say I wish you would reconsider. I understand you don't want to think about Celia lying to you. And you wouldn't have to dwell on that part. Just think about getting a new family."

And what if it turns out that the new family doesn't want me? she thought. What if I did get close to them and then it turned out that all this evidence about Amelia and Noah was really just gossip? How could I bear such a loss?

Shivering at the questions in her mind, she shook her head. "I thank you, Lonnie. For all the trouble you've gone to…to let me know about this. But I've got my baby to think about. And I don't really want my life to change. It's okay like it is. I'll be better off if I just let the whole thing drop. And so will the Ketchums."

"How could you know that?" he argued. "You've never met them."

"And they've never met me," she countered. "So they can't be so all-fired sure they want me in their family. Just like I can't be sure I'd want to be in theirs."

"You could have a trial run," he reasoned.

She clutched the hood of her coat beneath her chin. "Real families don't have trial runs. They're just stuck with each other. And sometimes they're miserable. That's not for me. I'd rather be alone."

Lonnie studied her wretched expression and wished there was some way he could change her mind, to make her see she was turning her back on something precious. "Sometimes they're not miserable, though. Sometimes they're real happy."

Her eyes strayed away from his as she looked out

the windshield and sighed. "That's a chance I don't want to take."

Heavy disappointment flooded through him and he wondered whether his melancholy was because this was the last time he'd ever see Katherine McBride, or because she was giving up the chance of a lifetime. Either way, he wouldn't give up on her.

Reaching to the back pocket of his jeans, he pulled out his billfold and fished a business card from the contents. With a ballpoint pen, he scratched his name and home phone number across the back, along with the name of the motel he was staying at here in Fort Worth.

"Here's my home number and also where I'm staying tonight. If you change your mind before morning, call me at the motel. And if you change your mind later, call me at the house or my office. I'm usually always available."

Katherine looked at the card. If she had any sense, she wouldn't accept it. She'd break the connection between them completely. But to think of never seeing or talking to this man again was something she didn't want to contemplate, so she snapped the card from his fingers and thrust it into her coat pocket. She wouldn't look at it, she promised herself. Just knowing it was there would be enough.

She unsnapped the seat belt, then leaned across the expanse of the leather seat. There was a look of surprise and confusion on his face as she planted a soft kiss on his cheek.

"Goodbye, Lonnie. Have a safe trip home."

He stared in wonder while she opened the door and slid to the ground and then reality hit him and he jumped out of the truck to assist her.

"You don't think I'm going to let you go back up those stairs by yourself, do you?"

She smiled wanly at him as he took her by the arm. "I climb them every day by myself."

"Maybe you do. But I'm here tonight. And it's very dark."

The clouds were high and heavy, blotting out any iridescent light there might have been from the moon and stars. It was nice to have his big arm to cling to and the shelter of his body shielding her from the cold wind as they climbed the concrete stairs to the landing above. Yet as they walked to the door, all she could think about was that he was leaving and she'd never be close to him again. More than likely she'd never see him again. The thought saddened her like nothing had in a long, long time.

"Do you have your key?"

"Sure. Just a minute." She fumbled in her purse, then handed him the silver object. He quickly opened the door and she reached inside and flipped on the light.

"Would you like for me to go inside and check everything out?"

Tears gathered at the back of her eyes, making her feel like a complete fool. It had to be those damn hormones again. She wasn't a woman prone to tears. Not even in hard times.

"No, thank you, Lonnie. We have good security here. I'm sure everything is fine. You need to be on your way. You have a long drive ahead of you tomorrow."

She slipped her hand from his arm, and he looked at her with an almost pained expression.

"You're right," he told her. "I guess I'd better be

going. Goodbye, Katherine. It was nice meeting you. And I hope everything turns out okay for you."

She smiled at him and was surprised to find her lips were trembling. "I'm glad I met you, too, Lonnie."

He studied her face one last moment before he moved away from her and started down the stairs. Katherine swallowed hard at the lump suddenly choking her throat.

"Don't forget to call if you change your mind," he said over his shoulder.

Unable to utter a word, she lifted her hand in a simple wave, then hurried inside and shut the door behind her. Once she'd safely fastened the locks she took a step toward the couch. Then just as quickly, she groaned and turned on her heel.

With her nose pressed to the window, she peered down at the parking lot below. Lonnie's truck was pulling away from its parking slot and heading toward the street running adjacent to the apartment building. At the intersection, the brake lights winked brightly in the darkness and then merged into the line of passing vehicles. In a matter of moments the vehicle was lost in the traffic, and Katherine turned listlessly away from the window.

She didn't know why Lonnie's departure had left her feeling so melancholy. She'd only known him for twenty-four hours. A person couldn't form an attachment in that short a time.

Trying to put the sheriff out of her mind, Katherine switched on the television and went to the kitchen to make herself a cup of instant coffee. She should have invited Lonnie in for a cup and a few cookies, she thought, as she filled the teakettle with water. She'd knocked him out of having dessert at the restaurant.

Do you ever make homemade pies, Miss Katherine?

The memory of his question put a winsome smile on her face. He'd probably like apple or blackberry, she decided. Something with a kick that required lots of sugar. She'd like to do something personal for him, like baking a pie. Because she knew he would smile and compliment her and truly appreciate the effort she'd gone to. He was just that sort of man. The kind she'd always wished to meet someday.

Well, you met him, and now he's gone, she thought. And that was good. Now she could forget him and all the things he'd told her about the Ketchum family. About Amelia and poor Noah.

It was hard to believe the man was dead. Murdered! And why? Why would someone have killed old Noah? She should have asked Lonnie about that. But everything had been such a shock to her she hadn't been able to think straight, much less ask sensible questions.

The teakettle began to whistle and for the next few moments she concentrated on making the coffee. But as she carried the hot drink into the living room, Lonnie and the Ketchums returned to her thoughts.

With a heavy sigh, she sank into the armchair and rubbed a hand across her belly. It would be nice to have a family. Especially for the baby's sake. He'd grow up to have aunts and uncles and cousins and a sense of his roots. That would be good. It was important for a person to know where he came from.

These past two days she'd learned just how important. The idea that Celia might not have been her real mother had shaken the ground beneath her. It still shook, but she had to forget it. Get over it. She wasn't going to let Lonnie or the Ketchums turn her world upside down.

For the next fifteen minutes Katherine sipped her coffee and tried to focus her attention on the television screen. She was a news junkie, and normally she could lose herself in the events occurring around the world and across the nation. But tonight her interest lagged and several times she caught herself wondering if she'd made a big mistake by sending Lonnie away. She shouldn't be feeling lost without him. But darn it, she was!

Eventually Katherine muttered a frustrated oath and reached for the telephone. In seconds she heard Althea's voice on the other end of the line.

"Katherine! Is something wrong? You don't normally call this late in the evening."

Katherine bit down on her bottom lip. "I'm sorry, Althea. Were you getting ready for bed?"

"Gosh, no! It's not that late. I'm doing laundry, and Tom is out on call. Someone's furnace has gone out and in this freezing weather he didn't want them to have to wait until morning."

Althea's husband, Tom, worked as a heating and air-conditioning repairman. Since Katherine had gotten to know the couple, Tom's business had boomed. He'd already taken on two partners and was considering adding a third so it would free him up to spend more time with Althea and their young daughter, Julie.

"Oh. Well, I'm glad I'm not bothering you because I…I was wondering if I could come over and talk to you for a few minutes. I won't keep you up late. Promise."

"Of course you can come over. You don't even have to ask!" Althea exclaimed. "But Katherine, what's wrong? You sound distracted."

"I am distracted! But I don't want to get into it over the phone," she told the other woman.

"It's not the baby, is it?" Althea asked worriedly. "Do you need to go to the doctor?"

"No! No! It's nothing like that. I'll tell you when I get there," Katherine told her, then quickly hung up the phone.

Under normal conditions, the drive to Althea's house took about ten minutes. But tonight the street traffic was minimal and she made the trip in just a little over five.

As soon as she knocked on the door, Althea jerked it open and tugged her inside.

"You shouldn't be out in this weather, Katherine! And at night like this! If Julie hadn't already been in bed I could have driven over to your apartment."

Katherine waved a dismissive hand at her friend. "That part doesn't matter. I'm just glad I'm here. I'm feeling silly and I want you to tell me to stop it."

Frowning, Althea led her over to the couch. Katherine removed her coat and took a seat while her friend grabbed the remote control and turned down the sound on the television.

"What are you feeling silly about? Did Richard do something this evening before you left work? Or…" She paused and worriedly studied Katherine's pale face. "He didn't call you at home or anything like that, did he?"

Katherine quickly shook her head. "No. It's not Richard. And thank God he hasn't started bothering me at home. But I expect that to happen soon," she added dourly.

"Then what's this all about? It has to be something big, because it's like pulling teeth to get you over here for any sort of visit," Althea said.

With a long sigh, Katherine pushed a hand through her dark hair and looked around the cozy living room. There were signs of Althea and Tom's daughter all over the place: a Barbie doll on the floor near the fireplace, a box of crayons and a coloring book on the coffee table, a pair of small tennis shoes and a matching red sweater piled near the leg of the couch. The sights reminded Katherine all over again that Althea had a real family with a beautiful little daughter and a loving husband. And though her friend's house was modest, it was just the sort of home that Katherine had always wanted. Rooms full of love.

"It's that sheriff," she finally said. "He showed up again tonight. Just like I told you he would. And, Althea, he had roses. Roses!"

Althea scooted to the edge of her armchair. "Really? What was his reasoning for those?"

Katherine shrugged. "He thought I was upset with him. And I guess it was his way of apologizing."

A sly smile spread across the brunette's face. "Sounds like Tom could take lessons from this sheriff. But don't tell me you're upset because a man gave you roses!"

Katherine pulled a face at her. "No! That's just part of what happened. He, uh—" She paused and drew in a deep breath as she felt her face turning red. "He took me out to dinner. We ate and talked and then he asked me to go home with him to his ranch in Hereford."

Althea's mouth dropped open. "Go home with him! What kind of guy is this, Katherine? Are you really sure he's the sheriff of Deaf Smith County?"

Katherine's head bobbed up and down. "Positive. And he didn't mean go home with him in the sense you're thinking."

Disappointment crossed Althea's face. "Shoot. That takes all the fun out of it."

Groaning, Katherine lifted her eyes to the ceiling. "Althea, this isn't a time for jokes. I'm…I need your help. I'm miserable."

"Oh, honey," Althea said, her expression suddenly contrite. "I'm just trying to lighten your mood. I know this is serious. So what did you tell this sheriff? And why did he ask you in the first place?"

Katherine pressed fingertips against both her temples. "I told him that I couldn't go with him, of course. And he asked me because he has some fool notion that if I go out there to his ranch and rest and relax for a few days, I'll decide that I want to meet with the Ketchums. In other words, I guess he thinks he can talk me into meeting the family."

"And you told him you didn't want to meet the Ketchums?"

Katherine nodded glumly.

"Okay. So what's wrong? If you're completely sure you don't want to meet these people, then I don't see a problem. You're simply not going. That is what you want, isn't it?"

Dropping her hands from her forehead, she looked miserably at Althea. "I don't know. I believed that's what I wanted. But after Lonnie left I felt…well, I felt like I'd lost something. Something I might never find again. I know that sounds crazy, but I can't help it."

Rising from her chair, Althea went over to the couch and took a seat next to Katherine. Once she'd put her arm around the other woman's shoulders, she said, "It sounds to me like you need to go to this man's ranch. You're all mixed up and you need time to think. If he's offering you a place to stay, why not take him up on it? He sounds like a nice man."

He *was* a nice man, Katherine thought. That was one of the problems. With no effort at all, she could let herself fall for him. And that was the last sort of problem she needed at this time in her life.

"The baby is coming soon," Katherine reminded her.

"That's one more reason you need to go now. Before your little one gets here and you can't go."

"I can't just leave work," Katherine protested.

"You have maternity leave coming," Althea pointed out. "Start it a little early. Tell Richard your doctor advised you to get more rest."

"My doctor did advise me to get more rest."

As though that settled everything, Althea threw up her hands and jumped to her feet. "See? You'd be telling the truth. And," she added slyly as she stood smiling in front of Katherine, "you'd be getting away from your boss for a while. I know that would take some weight off your back."

Althea was right. It would be a relief not to have to face Richard every day. After a moment she said, "I'm scared. You're making a little sense."

Althea giggled. "Sometimes I do. Though Tom has his doubts." She sobered as she studied Katherine's face. "Look Katherine, I realize you don't want to think about Celia being your aunt or that Amelia and Noah might be your real parents. But how can you not think of it? And if this sheriff is a friend of the Ketchums then you could learn a whole lot about your family."

Katherine frowned. "They might not be my family. This whole story may be made up or simply a mistake. Then where would I be?"

Althea tilted her head to one side as she contemplated Katherine's question. "Well, you could always come back here to Fort Worth. Tom and I will always be here for you. No matter what happens with the Ketchums."

Tears stung Katherine's eyes. Having Althea was the closest thing she would probably ever have to a sister. Unless Lonnie was right about Victoria Ketchum. But Katherine didn't for one second count on that idea. If she really had brothers and a sister, Celia would have told her. She wouldn't have let Katherine continue to live a lie for all these years! Or would she?

Stifling a groan, she looked at Althea. "You're right about one thing. Every time I try not to think about the Ketchums and the story of my…well, my supposed parents, I only think of them more. Maybe it would be good for me to take time off and try to figure out what I'm going to do—or not do."

Althea slowly nodded. "You're not going to have any peace if you don't. And you sure wouldn't be much help at work."

Work! How nice it would be, Katherine thought, to be able to simply prop her aching legs up during the day at any time she chose to. It would be downright decadent to sleep until seven o'clock in the morning and not have to deal with the rush hour traffic as she drove to the courthouse. But most of all it would be a relief not to have to face Richard's suggestive smiles and well-meaning offers to help her out of her "predicament."

"You're right about that," she murmured absently.

"I can see the wheels in your head turning," Althea commented as she studied Katherine's thoughtful expression. "What are you thinking?"

Rising to her feet, she said, "I'm thinking I've got to go."

"Go! But you—"

"I'm going back to my apartment and call Lonnie," she interrupted Althea's protest. "To tell him I'm going with him."

Althea's eyes suddenly widened. "You're really going with the man?"

Katherine frowned at her. "Yes. Haven't you been encouraging me to do just that?"

Althea left the armchair and came to stand next to Katherine. "Yes. But now that you say you're really going, I'm suddenly worried. You say this Lonnie is nice, but you don't really know him. You might get yourself into a situation you'd rather not be in."

Only if she allowed herself to act like a fool over Sheriff Lonnie Corteen. And she wasn't about to do that, Katherine promised herself.

"If I do, I'll come right back home," she said simply.

Althea looked as though she was going to argue, but then her frown changed to a resigned smile. "You're right. This will be good for you. Just promise that if you need me you'll call."

Katherine nodded. "I promise. Now I'd better get home before it gets too late to call Lonnie."

Althea walked her to the door, and the two women parted with a hug. Ten minutes later Katherine was back in her apartment waiting for the motel switchboard to transfer her call to Lonnie's room. When he did finally answer the telephone his voice sounded tired and husky. Katherine's heart pitter-pattered beneath her breasts.

"Lonnie Corteen."

"Lonnie. It's me, Katherine. Did I wake you?"

At the sound of her voice, Lonnie scrambled to a sitting position on the side of the bed. "Er—no. You didn't wake me. I was just watching a little television."

There was a moment's pause and then she said, "That's good. I'm glad I didn't wake you. Uh, the reason I'm calling—"

"You've changed your mind. You've decided to go with me tomorrow."

A heavy release of air passed her lips. "How did you guess?"

"You wouldn't be calling me for anything else."

For some reason his words made her feel terrible, which didn't make any sense at all. She hadn't been invited to simply call him for a chitchat. This was business. They both knew that.

"Well, I…I got to thinking it over," she said. "And I decided a little trip might be just what I need right now. To get rested up before the baby comes."

Lonnie smiled. He couldn't help it. "That's good. I'm glad you changed your mind. And I think later on you'll be glad, too."

She hoped he was right. She'd never been an impulsive person. Usually she mulled over a problem for a long time before she ever made a decision. But tonight, after he'd walked away, she'd felt the urgent need to call him, to keep the slender thread between them from breaking. And she'd been ashamed to admit to Althea, and even herself, that spending more time with Lonnie Corteen had weighed heavily on her decision to travel to West Texas.

"When were you planning to leave?" she asked suddenly.

"Well, I was planning on getting away from Fort Worth before daylight. But naturally, if you're going with me, I can leave later."

Katherine bit down on her bottom lip as her thoughts whirled. "I'm going to need some time to get things in order with my job. And I'll need to speak to my doctor. I might be ready by noon or shortly after. Is that too late?"

Lonnie hated driving after dark, but if it meant she would travel with him, he could change his preferences.

"No. That's fine," he said quickly. "Just call me here at the motel whenever you're ready. Unless— Do you need some help packing or anything?"

Was he always going to be this nice? Katherine wondered. Didn't anything make him testy? After all, he was a man. He was supposed to be more selfish than this. At least, all the men she'd known put their needs and wants before any one else's. After a few days in his company, she'd probably find out Lonnie wasn't any different.

"Thank you, but I can manage. I'm already putting you out, anyway."

"I came here to Fort Worth to get you, Katherine. I'm happy you're letting me get the job done."

She was a job to him. If she could continue to remember that, her heart would be perfectly safe in his company.

"Is the bus station still there at Hereford? I'll need a way to get back home."

Not if the T Bar K in New Mexico became her home, Lonnie thought. But that was a big if and he didn't want to question or push her right now for any reason.

"Yes, it's still there. But don't worry about transportation to Fort Worth. If necessary, I can drive you back."

That would be entirely too much to ask of him, but she didn't say so. When the time came to leave his home, she could argue that point with him.

"All right. I'll see you tomorrow, then," she told him.

"Good night, Katherine. And I'm…very glad you've decided to go with me."

His husky voice rippled across the phone line and shivered down her spine.

"I am, too," she said softly, then hung up before he could hear the emotional tears in her voice.

Chapter Five

The next day Lonnie was still in a daze. As he paced around the small motel room and waited for Katherine's call, he continued to wonder what he'd gotten himself into.

A woman in *his* house! Eating at his table and sleeping in his bed. Well, not *his* bed, he mentally corrected, but the bed across the hall. And that was bad enough. What was he going to do with her?

Nothing Corteen, that's what! The woman was pregnant. She wasn't in any shape to be on the hunt for a man. And even if she was, he wasn't looking to fill the bill. Not that a woman like Katherine would look at him sideways, he thought wryly. She was all soft and pretty and intelligent. She could have most any man she wanted. And she wouldn't want a big, bumbling cowboy sheriff, who could count the number of his past girl-friends on one hand.

The loud ring of the telephone suddenly broke into Lonnie's thoughts and he dove at the instrument situated by the head of the bed. The receiver jostled from its cradle and clattered to the floor.

Biting back a curse, Lonnie scooped up the telephone and rammed it against his ear. "Lonnie Corteen here."

"Lonnie, it's me, Katherine," she said in a breathy rush. "I think I have everything ready to go. I'm sorry it's so late, but I had to speak to my doctor about making the trip. And then I had to deal with my boss about starting my leave."

He glanced at his wristwatch. In just a few minutes it would be noon. "Is there going to be a problem with your job? You leaving so unexpected like this?"

There was a slight pause and then she answered, "No. Everything is okay with my replacement."

"What about your doctor?"

She sighed. "He wasn't all that keen on the idea of me traveling. In fact, he advised me not to make the trip. But he didn't forbid it."

Concerned now, Lonnie sat down on the edge of the bed. "Katherine, maybe we should plan for you to travel later. If making the trip caused you or the baby any harm, I'd never forgive myself."

"It's not that the trip might make me or the baby ill, Lonnie. He's just afraid I'll go into early labor. But after I told him that I'd be traveling with a sheriff and that you would make sure I got immediate medical treatment if it was needed, he was okay with the whole thing."

Lonnie's gaze lifted to the ceiling. She certainly had much more confidence in him than he did. "Well, I'd certainly do my best to take care of you, Katherine. But if the situation was—" He didn't finish what he'd been about to say. He didn't want to scare her. He just wanted her to be aware of the risk she was taking. Car trouble could happen at any time to anybody. And there were long stretches of Texas plains where there was nothing but empty cornfields, herds of cows and a lone windmill here and there. He might be a county sheriff, but he couldn't conjure up medical help where there was none. "Well, I just want you to be sure you want to go," he finished.

"I do."

The two simple words were like the soft, playful thuds of a fist to his midsection. He wasn't quite sure if he loved the feeling or hated it.

Rising to his feet, Lonnie reached for his hat and levered it down on his head. "Okay, Katherine. That's all I need to know. I'll be over there to pick you up in a few minutes."

When Lonnie knocked on her apartment door a few minutes later, Katherine was all packed and ready to go. She let him in and gestured to the two small bags sitting on the floor near the couch.

"That's all I'm taking. I figure I won't need much for just a week's time."

Lonnie was glad to see Katherine had dressed warmly in a pair of cream-colored corduroys and a peach-colored sweater. The wind was fiercely cold, and if they had to get outside the truck for any reason he wanted her to be protected.

"What about your cats?" He looked at the two felines that were perched on the back of the couch, watching him with suspicious eyes. Apparently they'd already figured out they were being left behind and Lonnie was the reason.

Katherine glanced at her beloved pets. "I have a friend who's coming to pick them up after work. She'll take them to her house and let them stay there until I get back."

"You could take them with us," he offered. "I wouldn't mind them being in the house."

Katherine turned wide eyes on him. "That's kind of you, Lonnie. But I wouldn't dream of taking advantage of your hospitality in that way. They'll be fine with Althea. And maybe they'll appreciate me more once I get back," she added with a smile.

She had an angelic smile, Lonnie thought. Sweet and dreamy with an innocent charm that would almost make a person think she'd never kissed a man before. But all he had to do was look at her belly to see she'd done far more. And she was paying dearly for it now, he thought grimly.

Thrusting the sad thought from his mind, he reached for her coat on the arm of the couch. "Come on, we'd better get started before it gets too late. I'm not wild about driving after dark. You never know when there might be a deer or a stray cow or horse on the highway."

He helped her on with the coat, then grabbed up her bags. Once they were outside of the apartment, she made sure the door was locked safely and that everything on her to-do list was marked off.

"It's not really a very pretty day for traveling, is it?"

she commented as they descended the stairs. "The wind is freezing and the clouds look dark and heavy."

"I'm hoping the clouds will begin to clear as we head west," he said. "But I doubt that happens. The weather is supposed to turn bad by tomorrow evening."

He had offered her his arm before they started down the staircase. Katherine clung to it tightly, grateful for the support of his strong body.

"How long will it take to get to Hereford?" she asked. "If I remember right, it took several hours to drive from Canyon to here."

"Probably six and a half or seven. Want to change your mind?"

The two of them had reached his pickup truck and Katherine stood to one side of the door while he unlocked it with his key. Maybe she should change her mind, she thought, as he helped her into the cab. No doubt it was foolish for her to be heading off on a trip this late in her pregnancy. But she was tired. Oh, so tired. And it was like Althea had said, a week away from everything would do Katherine a world of good.

She frowned at him. "Last night you were gung-ho for me to go. Now you sound as if you want me to back out of the trip. Why?"

Because he was worried, Lonnie thought. Because it made him jittery to think he was giving this woman so much attention. And liking it in the process.

"I'm still gung-ho," he said. "Especially if it gets you and the Ketchums together."

She cast him a look of warning as he helped her up and into the cab. "I wouldn't count on that."

"Well, I wouldn't count it out, either," he murmured.

Without waiting for her to make any sort of reply, Lonnie shut the door and went around to take his seat behind the wheel. In moments they were out of the parking lot and heading for the major vein of traffic that would eventually lead them out of the city.

Katherine remained thoughtfully quiet as the big sheriff negotiated the truck through the lunch hour traffic. What was she doing anyway? she kept asking herself, as the skyline of Fort Worth slowly slipped behind them. She didn't want to meet Seth Ketchum. And she sure didn't want to think of the late Amelia Ketchum being her mother. So why was she heading west with a man she hardly knew?

From the lowered veil of her lashes, Katherine studied his profile and, as she did, she realized she had to be honest with herself. Something about the man had gotten to her. He'd charmed her with his simple talk and slow smiles. He'd made her want to dream, to think there was something better out there in the world for her, something precious that she dare not turn her back on.

"Are you okay?"

His question brought her head up, and she looked at him squarely. "Yes. I'm fine. Just thinking."

"Worrying, you mean?"

A tiny frown marred her forehead. "What makes you say that?"

"You look worried. You've looked that way ever since we drove away from your apartment."

She heaved out a sigh. "Well, it's not every day that I take off in the middle of a workday with a strange man."

"I'm not a strange man. I'm a sheriff. That ought to put your mind at rest."

Katherine made a helpless gesture with her hand. "That's not what I meant. It's just that I'm not normally impulsive. And I never take time off from work. This trip wasn't necessary, so I'm wondering if I've done the right thing."

A brief smile touched his rugged face. "Well, look at it this way, it probably won't hurt anything."

Her eyes widened. "Probably?"

Lonnie shook his head in disbelief. "Just a figure of speech, Katherine. Mercy, you need to calm down or I'm going to be delivering that baby on the side of the road."

Embarrassed color filled Katherine's cheeks. He was right. She couldn't stay in this state of turmoil the whole time she was away from Fort Worth. She needed to relax and enjoy being away from the everyday grind and having the opportunity to see new things. And even if Lonnie Corteen was the sexiest man she'd ever met, that wasn't a fact to fret over. He wasn't going to make a play for her.

"Lonnie, that letter you told me about. The one my mother had written to Amelia Ketchum. Do you still have it?"

The look on his face said her question had surprised him. "Sure. It's in my bag behind the seat. Why?"

Katherine shrugged, then turned her gaze out the window. They were getting out of the suburbs now. Farm and ranch land was beginning to spread out from either side of the major four-lane highway. "I suppose I should have read it that first night you came to the apartment. But I—to be honest with you, Lonnie, I was scared."

The brief glance he tossed at her was long enough to see the convulsive movement in her throat as she struggled to swallow. Her emotional tussle bothered him like hell. Not because he was softhearted and melted at the first sign of tears. No. A man couldn't be softhearted and be a county sheriff. But the uncertainty surrounding his own mother's disappearance made Lonnie appreciate a little of what Katherine was going through.

"I can understand that," he said. "Do you want to see the letter now?"

She shook her head. "No. Maybe later, after we get to your place." Katherine looked at him, her eyes a little pleading, a little wary. "Does it—does my mother talk about me?"

Lonnie nodded. "She does."

Her chin tilted firmly upward. "I'm not going to ask you what it says. I'll wait and read it for myself."

"I don't know what it says exactly," Lonnie explained. "I haven't read the letter. That's something private from Seth and his family to you."

Katherine studied him closely. "Oh. I just took it for granted—"

"Seth told me a little of what the letter contained. That's why I knew that Celia talked about you."

"Oh," she said again, then plucked at the corduroy fabric covering her knee. "Tell me about where you live."

She was changing the subject, a fact that Lonnie didn't bother to mention. There would be plenty of time later for him to bring up the subject of her family.

"My home is nothing special, Katherine. About a

thousand acres of rolling prairie, a few barns, and a little stucco house with two bedrooms. I raise a few cows. A few horses."

My home. Lonnie's two words brought a wry smile to Katherine's lips. She'd never thought of her apartment as a home. It was just a place to stay, to eat and sleep and live out her life until—until what? she wondered. Until something magical happened and some gallant knight came along and carried her off to his home where the two of them would have a happy-ever-after family? No. She, more than most women, knew things like that didn't happen. Not even with modern-day knights. A woman had to make her own home. She couldn't wait around for a man to do it for her. And Katherine was trying to do just that. If she stayed put at her job as Richard's secretary, her bank account would continue to grow. She'd be able to purchase a place in Fort Worth on a quiet, little street where her baby could grow up to attend a decent school with decent friends.

"Your home sounds very nice," she murmured.

A soft chuckle passed his lips. "I don't know if I'd go so far to say that. Just wait till you see how messy my house is."

"Oh, it couldn't be worse than mine." Turning slightly toward him, she studied him with interest. "I'm curious to know how you find time to have cows and horses. I figure a county sheriff is normally a busy man."

"I'm always tight on time," Lonnie agreed. "But I have a unit of good deputies that don't have to call me when any little thing happens. They can handle things first and tell me about it later. That takes a whole lot of stress off me."

He didn't look like a man who got stressed over anything, Katherine thought. He looked like one of those easy-going men who never panicked in a sticky situation. She also sensed that if anyone riled him to anger, he would be tough as nails.

"Have you been a lawman for a long time?"

"Ten, nearly eleven years. I went to work when I was nineteen years old as a deputy for Ethan Hamilton down in Lincoln County, New Mexico."

"I didn't know deputies could be that young!" Katherine exclaimed.

An amused grin crossed his face. "Well, I guess I was kinda like Chester in *Gunsmoke*. I just had a penchant for being a lawman. And Ethan was nice enough to give me a chance. He taught me a lot about enforcing the law, and I'll always be grateful to him."

"Lincoln County," Katherine mused aloud. "Isn't that where the famous range wars occurred back in the 1800s?"

"That's it."

"You used to live there—in New Mexico?"

"Yeah," he answered. "That's where my mother left me. With a family in Carrizozo." He shrugged. "So that's where I grew up and that's where I stayed until I was twenty-four."

"Why did you leave?" Just as soon as the question was out, she wished that she could take it back. She was getting too personal. Learning all about this man wasn't a smart thing to do. But she was interested in how he had become the person he was now.

He kept his gaze on the traffic. "Oh, by then I'd become Ethan's chief deputy, but I knew if I stayed in Lincoln County that would be as far as I could move up on the roster. Everybody down there loves Ethan. He'll be the sheriff there until he dies or retires. Whichever comes first."

"You could have run against him in the sheriff's race. You might have won," she suggested.

His head twisted around and he stared at her as if she'd just said a string of vulgar curse words. "There's no way on earth I would've run against Ethan! He's one of my very best friends. If it wasn't for him—well, I'd hate to think where I'd be today without him. I don't repay my friends by stabbing them in the back."

Katherine straightened her shoulders. "I wasn't suggesting you did. I just assumed you would've liked to be sheriff down there. I'm sure this friend of yours would have understood if you'd tried a shot at his job."

"Oh, yeah. He would have understood. But I couldn't have lived with myself. And anyway, I wouldn't have won the election. Ethan comes from a wealthy, well-known family. I was just, well, a regular guy. I had friends and I was liked. But I didn't have the clout. If you know what I mean."

Katherine knew very well. She'd never had clout, either. Being raised by a single parent who'd been forced to count her pennies, Katherine hadn't been exposed to the higher social circles. But that had never bothered her. She wasn't the high-society type. In fact, she'd always felt uncomfortable and out of place around the rich folks in Canyon. And when Lonnie had talked about the Ketchums' wealth, her mind had pretty much closed the door on them. She didn't belong with that type of people. Maybe in the next few days she could make Lonnie understand that.

"Yes. I do know." She glanced out the window to see they were well and truly away from the city now. Ahead of them on the far horizon, gray clouds swept down to meet the highway. Katherine hoped it wasn't the sign of ominous things to come. "How long have you been sheriff of Deaf Smith County?"

"About five years. I worked there as a deputy first and then decided to run for the sheriff's office. That's when Seth Ketchum stepped in to help me get the recognition I needed to be elected."

She thought about that for a few moments. "So. You owe Mr. Ketchum a lot."

Lonnie nodded. "He's like Ethan—he's a good man."

Lonnie was a good man, too, Katherine mused. That's why he was going to this length to help a friend. He certainly wasn't taking her to his home because he *wanted* her there. If she could remember that, she'd make it through the next few days without a scratch.

Once they reached the outskirts of Wichita Falls, Lonnie stopped at a fast-food restaurant to give Katherine a bathroom break and to buy two cups of coffee to take on the road with them.

Katherine had always been a good traveler. Normally, she could drive for hours without getting tired. But as the afternoon wore on and the miles slipped behind them, her back began to hurt and her legs ached. By the time they were nearing Amarillo, she was constantly shifting in the seat, searching for a more comfortable position.

"Why are we stopping here?" Katherine asked, as Lonnie pulled into a large parking lot.

He made a motion toward one of the buildings in front of them. It was a Mexican restaurant and from the looks of things, a rather busy one.

"I've eaten here before. It's a good restaurant. And I know you have to be ready to eat and rest."

Surprised, Katherine looked at him. "But I thought you wanted to get home as early as possible?"

"It's already dark. Hurrying now won't help matters. And you're tired. A little break might help us both."

While he parked the truck, Katherine pulled on her coat, dabbed on a bit of lipstick and sent the quick flick of a brush through her hair. When Lonnie came around to the door to help her down, she was ever so grateful for the support of his arm.

"Oh, my back. It feels like someone has been whacking it with a two-by-four," she said with a groan. Stretching her shoulders, she planted both hands at the base of her spine and pushed. For a few moments she felt relief.

"Here," he said as they started walking toward the entrance of the restaurant. "Let me see if I can help."

Katherine groaned with pleasure as his hand came against her back and rubbed through the thickness of her coat. He seemed to know exactly where her muscles were aching and she wondered faintly if he'd been around a pregnant woman before. He'd said he'd never been married and he had no siblings. Maybe he'd had a pregnant girlfriend, she thought, as they approached the entrance. But that wouldn't be the case, Katherine decided. If Lonnie Corteen had ever had a pregnant girlfriend, she would now be his wife. He was just that sort of man. Unlike Walt, he wouldn't leave the responsibility of raising his child to anyone else.

"I'm sorry I've been such a whiner," Katherine apologized. "You must be getting sick of it."

Chuckling under his breath, he stopped the massage and opened the door to the restaurant. "You haven't been whining, Katherine. Considering your condition, I think you've been making it like a regular trooper."

He ushered her inside the blessedly warm interior of the restaurant where the two of them were quickly greeted by a hostess who led them to an annex off the main dining room. Even though most of the tables were filled, the smaller area was quiet, the conversations around them muffled. Katherine wasn't even trying to pick up on the words the couple behind them were exchanging, but, her ears perked with interest when she caught the phrase "winter storm approaching the panhandle."

Leaning across the table, Katherine spoke under her breath, "Lonnie, the couple behind us were just saying there's an ice storm coming."

Lonnie nodded. "I watched the weather on television today before I left the motel. The storm is predicted to hit by morning. If it wasn't for the chance of being caught in ice or snow, I'd find a motel and let you rest here tonight."

With a dismissive wave of her hand, she hoped she could hide the weariness in her voice. "Don't worry about me. It can't be too far now. I'll make it."

He smiled at her and there was a light in his eyes that said he was proud of her, that he commended her tenacity. The notion caused a sudden surge of pleasure to spiral through her, and Katherine found herself wondering why his approval was so important. She'd had other men compliment her for one reason or another. But somehow it was different coming from Lonnie. He was a sincere man. At least, from what she'd seen so far, she believed he was sincere. And he wasn't trying to charm her for his own gain. He was simply being himself.

"Well, if you don't feel well enough to travel after we eat, just tell me. We'll get a room and say to hell with the weather."

He turned his gaze back to the menu in his hands and Katherine was relieved. She could feel her cheeks growing hot and no doubt red. Just thinking of being in a motel room with Lonnie was enough to heat her senses.

She said, "Oh, no. We don't want to get stranded. And I'll be all right. I'd much prefer to go on to your house."

He glanced up from the menu and gave her a brief, encouraging smile. "We're only about an hour away from my ranch now, Katherine. We'll be there soon."

Once they finished their meal, the two of them didn't tarry in the restaurant. Lonnie paid the check, then helped her on with her coat. Out in the parking lot, the wind was whipping fiercely from the northwest. As Lonnie assisted her back into the truck, Katherine thought she felt a few drops of something moist hit her face, but she didn't mention it to Lonnie. Like he said, they were only an hour away. They could travel that before the storm hit.

Thankfully, the weather between Amarillo and Canyon remained dry, but just as they departed the Canyon city limits and headed south, drops of white mushy ice began to splatter the windshield.

Leaning forward in the seat, Katherine studied the dark glass in front of her. "Is that snow?" she asked anxiously.

"Looks like it." He turned on the windshield wipers. The rubber arms pushed crystals of ice to the bottom of the glass. "Damn it!" he muttered. "The storm must be moving faster than the weather service anticipated. I just hope we don't hit ice. Snow I can deal with."

Katherine pushed her nose against the passenger window and peered into the darkness. She couldn't see anything but the occasional light from a distant house. To the front of them, beneath the high beams of the headlights, the snow was growing thicker each second.

"Does your truck have four-wheel drive?" she asked hopefully.

His gaze focused on the highway, Lonnie nodded. "Yes. And that will help in the snow. But nothing helps on ice. Except maybe tire chains, and I don't have any of those with me. I wasn't expecting to stay in Fort Worth but just a night—and, well, I didn't bring any chains along."

Katherine suddenly felt awful. This man had already sacrificed his time and money to track her to Fort Worth. If she hadn't been so contrary about coming out here with him, they could have left yesterday and missed this dangerous storm.

"I'm sorry, Lonnie. Looks like I've gotten you into a mess," she said glumly.

He shot her a wry smile. "Don't be silly. You didn't get me into anything."

He'd gotten himself into this situation, Lonnie thought. In the first place, no one, including Seth, had *made* him go to Fort Worth to find Katherine. No one had made him stay there an extra day. And when she'd called and asked him to wait until she could travel with him today, he could have said no. He could have told her it was too late, that she'd missed her chance. But he and God both knew he couldn't have done that to her. Or to himself. Because once he'd heard her voice on the phone, telling him she was going home with him, he'd been filled with a gladness that had saturated his entire being. It was a scary admission. Especially for a man who'd done nothing in the past but strike out with women.

She let out a shaky breath. "Do you...think we'll be okay?"

He favored her with another smile. "Sure, Katherine. Don't worry. We might slip and slide a little. But I'm going to get you there safely. Come hell or high water," he chuckled as he attempted to allay her fears. "Or maybe I should have said hell and a snow bank."

She smoothed a weary hand across her brow, and Lonnie glanced back toward the highway. He didn't want her to see the uneasiness he felt. It would only upset her. And in her condition that was the last thing she needed.

"Maybe I should turn on the radio and try to find a weather report," she suggested.

Lonnie nodded. "Good idea. But before you do that, dig my cell phone out from under the passenger seat and I'll call my office in Hereford to see how the weather is there. It could be that we've just hit a snow shower and we'll drive out of it in a few minutes."

Once she'd fished the instrument from beneath the seat, she turned on the power and pushed the digits he called out to her. After it began ringing, she handed him the phone.

Lonnie knew something was amiss when a dispatcher answered his private line. Under normal conditions a deputy always took his calls.

"Scarlett?" he asked, recognizing the young woman's voice. "What in hell is going on down there?"

"Sheriff Corteen, is that you?"

"It is. I'm on Highway 60, just west of Canyon."

"Oh," she said with obvious disappointment. "I was hoping you were home. We tried you there and tried your cell phone, but you didn't answer."

Lonnie frowned. "I didn't have it turned on. I told Lester this morning that I'd be coming home tonight. So what's the matter?"

"Uh, well, it's just—" The telephone shrilled in the background, interrupting the female dispatcher. "Just a minute, Sheriff."

Lonnie looked over at Katherine and frowned. "They're having some kind of trouble. I—"

The dispatcher suddenly came back on the line, and Lonnie turned his attention to the voice in his ear.

"Sorry, Sheriff, but it's hell here right now. Ice has covered everything and there are fender benders everywhere. Plus, there are two serious wrecks out on the highway south of town. Ambulances are trying to get to the scenes now. All your deputies are working and it's the same with the city police."

"It's that bad?"

He could feel Katherine's anxious gaze bore into the

side of his face, and he cursed himself for not choosing his words better. No doubt she was listening carefully to every word he uttered. But there wasn't any way he could sugar coat what was ahead of them. A few more miles down the road and she was going to see for herself.

"Real bad," Scarlett answered. "The New Mexico and Texas Highway Patrol have issued travel warnings for people to stay off the roads. If it keeps up, they might even close I-40 from Tucumcari to Adrian."

He glanced grimly over at Katherine. She was staring out the windshield at the pellets of ice reflected in the beam of their headlights. The woman had to be exhausted, he thought. He desperately wanted to get her home and settled safely in a warm bed.

"Do you have any idea how much of Highway 60 is iced over?"

"No. Maybe—" The phone rang again to cut off the dispatcher's words.

"Scarlett? Isn't anyone there to help you?"

The dispatcher answered, "I, uh, just a minute, Sheriff."

While she worked the other phone, Lonnie said to Katherine. "I'm afraid it's bad news. We're going to be hitting ice soon."

Katherine glanced at him with dark, worried eyes. "I'm not surprised. It looks like we've run into a wall of sleet right now."

Already Lonnie was being forced to slow the truck's speed. Soon they would be traveling at a crawl.

"Are you holding up okay?" he asked Katherine.

She nodded bravely and gave him a tired smile. "Fine. Just a little back ache from all this riding."

He was about to tell her not to worry when Scarlett suddenly came back on the line.

"Sorry, Sheriff," she apologized again. "Lester is supposed…to be…with me. But he's having trouble getting…on…ice."

"My phone is breaking up, Scarlett. I'll try to call later."

He pushed the off button and tossed the instrument to the floorboard. Katherine leaned back in the seat and placed a protective hand over her mounded stomach.

"Scared?" he asked.

She looked at him and tried to smile. "Not with you."

Lonnie's heart swelled until he thought his chest would burst. And before he could stop himself, he reached over and took hold of her hand.

"We'll get through this, Katherine. Together."

Chapter Six

The next two hours were a living nightmare. The snow turned into rain, which quickly froze on everything it touched. Lonnie was forced to slow the truck to a virtual crawl. And even then, the vehicle slid this way and that over the heavy sheet of ice glazing the highway.

Katherine tried to relax, but it was impossible with the truck either heading for the ditch or the opposite side of the road. Their only saving grace was the lack of traffic. They'd met only a handful of cars heading north. And from their creeping speed, it was obvious they were having the same sort of problem that she and Lonnie were experiencing.

By the time they reached the turnoff to Lonnie's ranch house, Katherine was shaking with fatigue.

"Thank God," Lonnie said as he maneuvered the

truck onto the gravel road leading up to the house. "We should be there in a minute or two."

"I've never been so glad to get somewhere in my life," she told him.

Regret brought a twisted frown to his face. "I really got you into something, didn't I?"

She tried to laugh, but she was so tired the sound came out more like a croak. "I think it's the other way around. I really got you into something."

"I'm sure you're wondering why you ever agreed to come on this trip," he said.

A wry smile touched her lips. "I would have been wondering that even if we hadn't got caught in an ice storm."

Two minutes later, he pulled the truck to a stop next to a small stucco house with a ground-level porch running along the front. Since the weather made it difficult to see, Katherine couldn't tell much about the place, but she could make out a huge hardwood tree of some sort standing at one corner of the building and two tall cedars directly in front of the truck. The branches of evergreens were so heavy with ice, Katherine wondered how the limbs kept from snapping. As for the huge shade tree, she could only hope it didn't topple onto the house.

"Don't try to get out until I come around to help you," Lonnie ordered. "I figure it's going to be heck standing up out there."

Katherine nodded and he climbed out of the truck. As he carefully worked his way around the hood of the vehicle, she wearily pulled on her coat and picked up her handbag.

When Lonnie opened the passenger door, pellets of ice and wind smacked her in the face. Beneath her chin she gripped the edges of her collar together and tried to keep her teeth from chattering.

Lonnie leaned inside the open door and his big frame blocked the ice and wind. "If you'll pardon my language, Katherine, it's slick as hell out here. You're going to have to hold on to me and we'll inch our way to the house. Are you up to it?"

She nodded. "I'll do my best to stay on my feet."

His frown was full of concern and regret. "I wish I could carry you. But I'm afraid if I try that, I'll slip and drop you."

She reached for his hand. "Don't worry, Lonnie. We'll make it. Just let me hang on to you."

"I wouldn't dream of letting you go," he said. Putting his other hand beneath her elbow, he gently helped her down to the ground.

As soon as Katherine's feet hit the ice, she slipped, but thankfully it was straight into his arms. Her cheek landed against his chest, and for a moment as he steadied her, her face was nestled warmly in his down jacket. The pleasant scent of him was embedded in the fabric and for a wild second or two, she longed to push the fronts of the jacket apart and circle her arms around his waist.

"Are you steady? Think you can go now?" he asked.

His questions jerked her back to reality quicker than even the icy wind could have, and she looked up at him and nodded. "I'm ready."

Before they took any steps, Lonnie wrapped his arm securely around the back of her waist and then with his free hand, he took a firm grip on her forearm. Katherine could feel the iron strength of his muscles against her and she realized if she were to slip, he wouldn't allow her to fall.

"Just take it slow and steady," he instructed as the two of them took baby steps toward the porch.

"You left the truck door open," she said. "It's going to get wet inside."

"Don't worry about the truck. I'll get to that later."

The porch was made of concrete and was much slicker than the bare ground had been, but they managed to make it to the door without any mishaps.

Once Lonnie guided her into the warm house, Katherine could feel her legs turning mushy, and she gripped Lonnie's arm for all she was worth.

"Oh, dear, I'm so...tired," she said weakly. "Could you help me to your couch?"

His answer was to quickly bend down and scoop her up into his arms. "Put your arms around my neck, Katherine. I'm going to carry you to bed."

Bed! At the moment she was so exhausted she'd even be willing to share the mattress with him, she thought, as she curled her arms around his neck and buried her face there.

He took long strides through the house, which was dark but blessedly warm. After several twists and turns, he paused and fumbled with a switch just inside the door.

Light flooded the room, and she caught a glimpse of a bed with four tall, skinny posts and a white bedspread.

When he laid her down on the soft mattress, she sighed with weary relief. "I'm sorry I'm being such a burden," she said. "I guess the trip took more out of me than I thought."

He sat on the side of the mattress. "The last two hours were rough. *I'm* even drained." He motioned for her to rise up. "Let me help you out of your coat."

Placing her palms flat against the mattress she pushed herself to a sitting position, and Lonnie helped her ease the coat off her shoulders. Once he'd placed it on a nearby wooden chair, he came to stand beside the bed. "I'm going to go get our things from the truck. After that, I'll find us something to eat and drink. You just lie here and don't get up. Unless you need to go to the bathroom. It's right over there." He pointed toward one corner of the room where a door stood partially open.

She nodded in agreement and he started to move away from the side of the bed. Quickly Katherine grabbed his hand, and Lonnie paused to look down at her, his brows arched in question.

"I just wanted to know if you're always this good to everybody?"

His lips curved faintly as his eyes wandered gently over her pale face. "I couldn't tell you. I've never had anyone to be good to, Katherine."

He left the room and Katherine blinked as tears collected at the back of her eyes.

I've never had anyone to be good to.

At one time Katherine had believed she'd had someone. But then Walt had walked out on her and left her all alone, except for the baby growing inside her.

It wasn't good to be alone. She'd learned that when her mother had died and even more these past months she'd been pregnant. That was one of the reasons she'd decided to come out here with Lonnie Corteen. Because she hadn't felt so alone when she was with him. And because he'd offered her the hope of having a family. Not a family with him. But a family with the Ketchums. She had to keep reminding herself of that. Otherwise she was headed for a heartache she might not ever get over.

Several minutes later, Lonnie appeared in the room with a plate of food and a cup of coffee. Katherine sat on the side of the bed, and he dragged up the wooden chair and placed the small meal in front of her. There were a few other people, like Althea, who cared for her well-being, but it just wasn't the same as it was coming from this man with his bashful, sexy smile.

"We just ate at Amarillo, Lonnie. I really didn't need anything else. And I could have gone to the kitchen. There's no need for you to wait on me like I'm a queen or something," she protested.

"I'm not treating you like a queen. Just a pregnant woman." He stood at the edge of the bed and peered at her closely. "Katherine, you don't look so good to me. Are you sure you're all right?"

The concern in his voice brought a lump to her throat, but she did her best to smile at him. "Other than being tired, I have a few twinges in my back. But I'm sure it's from all that riding today. And I know the baby is fine. He's moving around like a kick boxer. Here, feel." She reached for Lonnie's hand and placed it palm down on the lower portion of her stomach.

His eyes widened as the movement of the baby rippled beneath his fingers. "Hey, that's something," he murmured. "What does it feel like to you? Does it hurt?"

A wan smile tilted her lips. "No. Not unless he really gets to pushing, and then it gets uncomfortable."

Her eyes met his, and he realized he'd gone on touching her for far longer than necessary. But she didn't seemed to be objecting, and his fingers lingered for a few seconds more before he slowly eased his hand away from her belly and stepped back from the bed.

"You, uh, still keep calling the baby a he," Lonnie said as he tried to hide the sudden awkwardness he felt at being so personal with her. "You really are convinced it's a boy."

Katherine smiled impishly. "Yes. But if I'm wrong, I'd take a girl, too."

"I'll just bet you would." And so would he, Lonnie thought. He'd love to have a daughter and a son. Maybe even three or four kids. He'd grown up without any parents or siblings and during that time he'd vowed he was going to make up for it by having a big family of his own someday. But then he'd gotten old enough to realize he needed a wife for such things and coming by one of those wasn't easy. Not if a man did it right. And after his fiasco with Ginger he wasn't at all sure he could ever get it right.

Katherine's eyelids began to droop, and he decided he'd lingered in her room long enough. On his way to the door he said, "I'm going to get myself a bite to eat and head for bed. If you need anything I'll be right across the hall."

"Thank you, Lonnie. Good night."

He paused on the threshold and glanced back at her.

Katherine smiled tiredly at him and he wondered how she could be so pleasant with him after he'd put her through such a trying trip. Most women would have been howling mad.

"Good night, Katherine. I'll see you in the morning."

She'd see him in the morning. Somehow knowing that made her bone-deep weariness seem only like a little discomfort and as he closed the door behind him, Katherine realized she'd made a big mistake coming out here to West Texas. She was falling for a man she couldn't have.

Someone was calling his name, but who? It was a woman's soft voice and it sounded sweetly familiar, like a pleasant song he often hummed.

"Lonnie! Are you awake?"

Sitting upright in the bed, Lonnie searched the shadows of the room until he spotted Katherine's silhouette moving in the open doorway. The sight sent his heart pounding with fear.

"Katherine. Is something wrong?" he asked in a voice rough with sleep.

She stepped into the room, and he reached over and switched on a small lamp by the head of the bed.

"I don't know," she said in a small, strained tone. "I…think I'm going into labor. The pains start in my belly and go around to my back. And they haven't let up since they started."

Wide awake now, Lonnie swung his legs over the side of the bed and reached for his jeans lying on the floor. "How long has this been going on?"

She shrugged. "Oh, about thirty minutes, I think. I'm not sure."

"Thirty minutes!" He jumped to his feet and at the same time hiked his jeans up over the white boxer shorts he was wearing. "Why didn't you wake me when it started?"

She made a helpless gesture with her hands. "Because I didn't think it was anything. I ate all that Mexican food and then I ate a little of that stuff you brought me. I thought it was my stomach…" The remainder of her words trailed away as her features twisted into a tight grimace. Then suddenly she clutched her lower abdomen. "Oh!" she gasped. "Oh, my goodness! Lonnie!"

Just as he reached for her, a flood of water splattered the floor and pooled around her feet. Lonnie was quick to recognize the liquid wasn't water. It was amniotic fluid. And from what he knew about birthing, that meant the baby was surely on its way.

"Katherine! Oh, God!" Swinging her into his arms, he carried her to his bed and placed her on the mattress. "You must be going into labor. I'll get the phone and call an ambulance."

Her eyes flew to his face, and Lonnie couldn't mistake the fear he saw in them. "The ice storm," she said. "Do you think an ambulance can make it out here?"

He didn't want her to think about that now. *He* didn't want to think about it.

"I don't know," he admitted. "Let me call first."

He hurried out to the living room and picked up the telephone, but before he could punch in the number, he realized there was no dial tone. Apparently some of the lines had fallen under the weight of the ice!

Slamming the useless receiver back on its hook, Lonnie rushed to the kitchen and found the cell phone in one of the bags he'd carried in from the truck before he'd gone to bed.

Quickly he pushed the power button on the instrument, only to have his hope dashed when the phone refused to give him a usable signal.

His eyes darted frantically around the room as his mind turned at a chaotic speed. Think, Lonnie! Improvise!

Suddenly he groaned with disbelief. Along with the two-way radio in his truck, he also had one set up in a corner of the living room he used for office space.

Sprinting back to the living room, he quickly powered up the radio and felt an immense sense of relief when the ambulance dispatcher responded.

"Yes, I can hear you, Sheriff Corteen, this is Pete, how's everything out your way? Iced in yet?"

Recognizing the young man as a longtime acquaintance, Lonnie barked back, "Hell yes, I'm iced in! And I need an ambulance sent out here. On the double. A woman is having a baby."

The dispatcher spluttered. "But…but, Sheriff, all the medical vehicles are out! There've been some serious car accidents out on Highway 60. Folks have been injured."

"I know about the accidents, Pete. But surely there's something left around there! The woman has gone into labor!"

"I think—I have the feelin' you'd better try to drive her in yourself," the dispatcher suggested. "Babies are unpredictable. You might not have time to wait."

The roads had been nearly impassable when he and Katherine had traveled over them a few hours earlier.

He didn't expect they'd gotten any better. Not when he could hear sleet striking the windows at this very moment. Damn it! What was he going to do?

"I don't think it's possible for me to drive," he said, then quickly thanked the dispatcher and hung up.

Back in his bedroom, he found Katherine writhing in pain. Fear shot through him like an unexpected bolt of lightning, and he hurried to her side.

The moment he touched her cheek, she realized he was in the room, and she took his hand and urged him down on the bed. Carefully Lonnie took a seat on the edge of the mattress and leaned over her.

"Is...the ambulance coming?"

Beads of perspiration had formed along her upper lip and forehead. Since the room was cool, he figured the sweat had to be a result of her pain.

"Uh, not right now. They're all busy. But they'll send one as soon as it's free."

A moan of despair slipped from her throat, and Lonnie was suddenly hating himself. He'd gotten Katherine into this predicament. Now he couldn't even help her out of it.

"I can't wait, Lonnie! The baby is coming. I can feel the pressure!"

The sound of panic was threaded through her words, and Lonnie understood that was the last thing she needed if the two of them were going to bring her baby safely into this world.

Since she was still gripping his left hand, he used his right to wipe the disheveled hair from her damp brow.

"Calm down, Katherine. Everything will be all right."

Her gaze latched desperately on to his. "Are you going to drive me into the hospital at Canyon?"

With a rueful expression, Lonnie shook his head. "That would be impossible, Katherine. It's been freezing rain ever since we got here. The roads could have only gotten worse. I can't risk stranding you out in the cold. If the baby was born—well, it wouldn't be good." He stroked the top of her head. "Do you really think it's coming soon?"

She nodded earnestly, and tears began to roll down her cheeks. "It's all my fault. I should never have come out here. I should have thought of my baby first. But I was…I mean…I thought maybe if I did meet the Ketchums, then he might have someone later…like cousins and uncles and aunts." She closed her eyes and swallowed hard. "But that was foolish thinking 'cause it just wasn't meant for me to have a family and now…if I lose this baby I'll not have anybody."

Tears continued to ooze from beneath her closed eyelids. Lonnie wiped them away with his thumb and wondered how he could live if something were to happen to this beautiful woman and her baby. But he couldn't dwell on that dark possibility. They were in his hands now and he was going to try his damnedest not to let them down.

"Shh. Don't even think such thoughts," he admonished firmly. "I'm going to take care of you. I won't let anything happen to you or the baby."

Her eyes opened and she looked at him doubtfully. "But you—"

"I've delivered a baby before," he interrupted. "A few years back, when I was just a young deputy. But I still remember how things work."

Relief flickered in her green eyes. "You've done this before?" she asked hopefully.

He nodded just as another pain doubled her over. Lonnie quickly disentangled his hand from hers and rose to his feet. "I'm going to go clean my hands and get some towels," he told her. "Just try to relax and not worry."

That was more easily said than done, Katherine thought, as Lonnie hurried out of the room. She'd never felt such excruciating pain in her life. The pressure on her pelvis felt as if she were being ripped apart. Yet above her physical pain was the sheer terror that she was going to have her baby right here in Lonnie's bed. Without painkillers. Without a doctor!

But she wasn't alone, she fiercely reminded herself. Lonnie was with her. And she trusted him. If she could have anyone, other than a doctor with her, it would be him. He was calm and steady and, being a sheriff, he'd dealt with crises. And this was definitely a crisis.

The bedroom door creaked, and through a fog of pain Katherine realized he'd come back into the room, carrying several towels and a shallow bowl. After he removed the plate of her bedtime snack from the chair, he placed the things on the seat and positioned the whole thing closer to the edge of the bed. From the shallow bowl, he wrung out a white washcloth and began to bathe her hot face.

The water was cool and heavenly against her skin, and her eyes flickered gratefully up to his. "That feels so good."

His smile was gentle as he glanced down at her. "I'm glad. Have the pains gotten closer? How do you feel?"

"Like I'm...oh, oh!" She stopped, gritted her teeth, then expelled a long breath. "I feel like I'm about to have a baby."

He folded the cloth and left it lying against her forehead. "I know this is embarrassing for you, Katherine, but I think I'd better have a look. The baby's head could be crowning."

She nodded and started to speak, but just then another fierce pain ripped through the lower portion of her body.

Lonnie didn't wait for her reply. He lifted the cover, and she turned her head to one side and drew up her knees as best she could. His hand closed around her knee before it slid inward to the intimate part of her thigh. His firm yet gentle touch was reassuring, and she instinctively parted her legs to allow him a better view.

"I'm not absolutely certain, Katherine, but I think I see the head. I believe it's time you started pushing."

"I...I'm not...sure I can," she sputtered between moans. "It hurts...sooo...bad, Lonnie!"

His hand cupped the side of her face that was exposed to him. Katherine turned her head and looked up at him with eyes that were glazed with pain and uncertainty.

"You can, honey," he urged. "You have to. You want your little guy to get here safe and sound, don't you?"

The pain ebbed away, and she whispered hoarsely, "More than anything. But I'm so tired."

He took the cloth from her forehead and washed her face again. "I know you're tired," he said softly, "but you've got to help the baby. He can't do it all on his own."

She bit down on her bottom lip as another searing pain racked her body.

Lonnie tossed the washcloth aside and grabbed both of her hands. "Here. Hold on to me and push. Now. Push hard!"

Gripping his hands, Katherine strained so hard the upper portion of her body lifted from the mattress. But once the pain subsided, she fell limply back against the pillows and panted weakly for breath.

Bending over her, Lonnie exclaimed, "That's doing it, Katherine! I can see more of the head now. It's covered in dark hair, just like yours!"

The awe and excitement in his voice filled her with a strange sense of elation, and she laughed and sobbed at the same time.

"Oh, Lonnie! Lonnie! Help me—I'm tearing apart!"

"Just a few more pushes, Katherine! That's all you need to do," he urged.

A few. Her head swam as agony enveloped her, but she tried to hold on to Lonnie's encouragement.

"I'll try," she whispered weakly.

The two words had barely gotten past her lips when another pain ripped across her pelvis. Lonnie urged her to push again, and this time the baby's head emerged.

Katherine let out a low scream as she strained to expel the infant. Lonnie finally managed to get a grasp on the baby's head and help it the rest of the way. Once the baby was safely in his hands, Katherine fell lifelessly back against the bed.

A glance at her white face had Lonnie fearing she had passed out, but he didn't have time to check on her condition. The tiny boy in his hands needed immediate attention.

As he grabbed a towel and began to administer to the baby, Katherine stirred.

"It's not crying, Lonnie!" she exclaimed hoarsely. "Why isn't my baby crying?" She attempted to rise up far enough to see, but she was too weak to even lift her arms from the mattress.

Her frantic pleas pierced Lonnie's heart. He hated knowing she'd had to suffer and worry through an experience that should have been special for her.

"It's all right, Katherine. I'm just trying to get the mucous out of his mouth. He looks like he's—"

Suddenly the baby sucked in a loud breath, and Lonnie laughed with sheer joy and relief. "There he goes. He's breathing, Katherine!"

Loud wails of protest erupted from the baby, and Lonnie decided he'd never heard a more beautiful sound.

Tears of relief slipped down Katherine's face. "Oh, thank God!"

"Thank God, is right," Lonnie reiterated as he reached for a sterilized knife to cut the umbilical cord. Afterward, he wrapped the newborn in a clean towel and then placed him in her arms.

"The doctor will tie that off and make him a nice belly button later," he assured her. A wide smile crossed his face he looked down at mother and baby. "Will you be all right for a couple of minutes while I go get some more things?"

"I think so. But Lonnie, I—" Pausing, she frowned and glanced down to the lower portion of her body. "It feels like I'm bleeding."

Instantly Lonnie yanked back the tangled covers. Shock rippled through him as he saw a bright red stain spreading beneath her. The afterbirth had already been expelled, seconds behind the baby. There wasn't any reason for her to be bleeding. Unless, dear God, she'd ruptured a blood vessel.

"Just be still," he ordered. "And calm. You're going to be all right."

Please God, let her be all right, Lonnie silently prayed. He couldn't imagine this world without her.

Quickly he pressed the flat of his hand down hard against her pelvis region and held it there. "You've probably just torn a spot," he tried to reassure her. "That boy of yours looks to be pretty hefty."

She glanced adoringly at the baby who was still crying lustily. And as she studied his precious face, another trail of emotional tears began to roll down her cheeks.

"He's so beautiful," she said in a fascinated whisper, and then her gaze turned desperately to Lonnie. "If something…happens to me you'll raise him, won't you?"

He was so shocked and overwhelmed by her question that for a few seconds all he could do was stare at her. "Katherine!" he finally scolded. "Nothing is going to happen to you."

Shaking her head, she reached for his free hand and squeezed his fingers. "Lonnie, promise me! I don't have anyone. There's no one I'd rather have raise him than you."

He was so stunned by her plea that he almost forgot to keep the pressure applied to her lower belly. "I'm sure you have friends, Katherine."

"Yes. But she already has a child—a girl. You would know how to raise a boy just right."

Lonnie had never felt so humbled in his life. The woman had gone through a trying birth, she believed she might be dying and she was talking about him being a good father! Didn't she understand that he didn't know anything about being a daddy? He barely remembered his own father. And, Carlos, the man who'd raised him, had seven children of his own. He hadn't had time to give Lonnie, or his other children, special one on one attention. He'd been too busy trying to keep them all fed and clothed.

Lonnie looked at her and the baby and tried to keep the fear he was feeling away from his smile. "I'm deeply flattered, Katherine. And I'd be honored—really honored—to raise your little one. And I would—if need be. But you're going to be fine. Trust me."

Glancing down, he could see the blood had stopped seeping, so he carefully lifted his hand. After a few long minutes passed, it appeared the flow had been stemmed completely.

"See," he announced with smug joy. "The bleeding has stopped."

Doubt filled her eyes. "Really?"

Still smiling, Lonnie nodded and eased gently up from the side of the bed. "Really. Like I told you, it was probably just a little tear. A few stitches and you'll be right as rain."

He went to the door and with his hand resting on the knob he paused to look back at her. "I'll be back in a few minutes, okay?"

She gave him a grateful little smile. "I'm not going anywhere."

He continued to stand there looking at mother and baby. In his wildest dreams, he'd never imagined a baby being born in his bed. He'd not even imagined a woman like Katherine in it, and for long moments he could only stare and wonder what it might be like if the two of them belonged to him.

Chapter Seven

More than an hour later, Katherine was clean and dressed in a fresh gown. Lonnie had also wiped the debris from the baby's skin and hair and now the two adults were inspecting everything about the sleeping newborn.

"He looks just like you, Katherine," Lonnie said in amazement.

Her face glowed as she looked down at her new son. "He does, sort of," she agreed. "How much do you think he weighs?"

Lonnie thoughtfully scratched his head. "Oh, more than a sack of flour. I'd guess about seven pounds."

"That big?"

Lonnie chuckled at her amazement. "A little earlier tonight you would have said he weighed twice that much."

A pretty pink color flooded her cheeks, and Lonnie

was relieved to see it. Earlier, right after the birth, she'd looked frighteningly pale.

"You know, I was expecting the labor pains to be bad. But no amount of planning could have gotten me ready for just how bad," she said. "I wasn't too good at giving birth. I'm sorry."

Picking up the baby's foot, he examined each perfect little toe. Everything about the newborn seemed like a miracle to him. Which every newborn was, he thought. But this one was even more wondrous and special to Lonnie because he'd helped bring it into the world. And most of all, it was Katherine's child.

"What are you talking about?" he softly admonished. "You were a real trooper."

Regret tugged down the corners of her full lips. "I screamed out. And I said some crazy things."

Pulling his gaze from the baby, Lonnie's guarded gaze traveled over her face. "You said if you died you wanted me to raise him," he said wryly. "I guess that does seem a bit crazy to you now. I'm not exactly a father figure."

Seemingly astonished that he should say such a thing, she stared at him, her lips parted. "I meant every word of that! And as far as I'm concerned, it still goes."

Happiness flooded through him like a warm, welcome rain and in the back of his mind, he realized he was headed for deep trouble. He could see it coming like a dark cloud, boiling and roiling out of control. This was the wrong woman for him to be setting his heart on. She had her own life back in Fort Worth. Her own baby to bring up. She wouldn't be interested in a county sheriff with far more guts than sense.

"I'm honored, Katherine. Real honored." He tried to

stop himself, but before he could, he leaned forward and pressed a kiss on her forehead. As he drew back from her, he murmured, "I hope you don't mind me doing that."

For long seconds her eyes studied his rugged features as though she wanted to remember them always and then she said, "The only thing I mind is that you didn't give me a proper kiss. A woman should have one of those after she gives birth to a son, don't you think?"

A real kiss? Suddenly his heart was hammering in his chest. "I think you're right," he whispered.

She smiled and as he touched his lips to hers, she decided the taste of him was like a hunk of sweet chocolate. Rich, tempting and oh, so delicious. Even after he raised his head, she wanted more. She wanted to feel his closeness, his strength, breathe in the unique scent of his hair and skin. What was wrong with her, she wondered wildly. Why was this happening now? All she should be thinking about was her new son. Yet without Lonnie she wasn't at all sure her baby would be nestled in the crook of her arm right now.

"Uh...I think it's time I should be thanking you," Katherine told him.

His brows lifted and the corners of his lips turned up with amusement. "I've never been thanked for a kiss before."

Her expression was suddenly serious. "I'm not talking about the kiss. I want to thank you for delivering my baby. I believe you saved both our lives."

She made him feel proud and important, two things he'd rarely experienced in his life and he could feel his chest swelling with emotions he'd never felt before.

"You're dramatizing things now, Katherine," he said humbly.

"No, I'm not. I couldn't have done it without you."

The soft glow in her eyes was directed straight at him and suddenly Lonnie felt very afraid. He'd hurt so badly when Ginger had left him. He didn't want to be put through that agony again. He didn't want to feel the deep humiliation that came with being unwanted. But every time he laid eyes on this woman he felt himself being drawn closer and closer to her.

The uneasy thoughts pushed him to his feet, and he walked across the room to peer out the window. Fat flakes of snow had taken the place of the freezing rain. Lonnie was relieved to see it. At least a four-wheel-drive and a set of chains could maneuver in the snow.

"Lonnie? Is something wrong?"

He looked over his shoulder at her and wondered how long it would take him to get used to the sight of her in his bed. *That's something you're not going to have to get used to, you fool. Katherine will be here for a few days and then she'll be out of your life.*

"No. Why?"

"You left your seat and you've been quiet for a long time."

He shrugged and since there wasn't any way he could tell her what was really going through his mind, he said, "I was just checking the weather. Snow is starting to cover the ice."

Sensing his withdrawal, Katherine's gaze drifted down to the baby sleeping in the crook of her arm. "I'm really sorry about all this, Lonnie," she said quietly.

He took a few steps toward the bed and then stopped.

"Why do you say something like that?" he asked with a frown.

A grimace momentarily tightened her lips. "Because I've caused you a lot of trouble. I've even ruined your bed."

She sounded so woeful he had to chuckle. "Oh, Katherine! Do you think I care about that? For Pete's sake, I can get another mattress. You and the baby can't be replaced."

"I'm serious, Lonnie. When you asked me to come out and stay a few days, you weren't asking for this kind of ordeal. And now—well, it will be a few days before me and the baby will be up to traveling back home. Until then, I don't want to impose on you."

He moved back around to the side of the bed, and her worried eyes followed his as he eased down beside her. Once he'd seen to her needs and the baby's, he left them long enough to change into a pair of faded jeans and a gray sweatshirt. The casual clothes were far different from the starched white shirt and Wranglers he'd worn in Fort Worth. He'd looked like a typical Texas lawman then, she decided. But right now he looked like a man she'd like to curl up with.

"Katherine," he said firmly, "you and the baby aren't going to be a burden. Besides, I'm the one who feels terrible about all this. I'm the one who put you through the grinding trip here—which obviously threw you into labor. It's all my fault. In fact, I wouldn't blame you a bit if you were pretty darn angry with me."

Angry! It would be far easier, Katherine thought, if she could be angry with the man. Instead she continued to marvel at the care he'd given her and her son, at the kindness he was still showing them.

"Lonnie, I'm not angry. And I don't blame you for anything. I think…it was just time for the baby to come. The doctor had already warned me it could happen earlier than expected. And he doesn't look a bit premature."

"He looks hefty and healthy to me."

She started to reply when she caught the sound of the phone ringing in another part of the house.

"I'll be right back," he assured her and then hurriedly went to answer the call.

In moments he was back with news for her. "That was the ambulance dispatcher. There's an ambulance on its way out here now."

Her eyes widened. "Now! It's too late for that. Didn't you tell them?"

Lonnie shook his head. "No. If they're able to navigate the snow, you and the baby need to go into the hospital tonight. He needs to be checked over and so do you."

Katherine knew he was right. But she didn't want to leave Lonnie or his bed. She felt safe now. Safe and wanted. A combination she didn't want to give up. At least, not tonight.

"I suppose you're right," she mumbled. "But I'm not keen on the idea. It feels pretty nice right here."

One corner of his mouth crooked upward. "Not crazy about hospitals, huh? Well, neither am I. Will it make you feel any better if I go with you?"

Hope glimmered in her green eyes and then just as quickly vanished. "You have to be exhausted, Lonnie. You need to stay here and rest. I'm sure you'll be needed at work tomorrow. Especially with this ice causing havoc with the roads."

Rising to his feet, he headed to the door. "I'll rest tonight. Don't worry about me. Right now I'd better get a few things ready for both of us."

Twenty minutes later, the emergency vehicle arrived. After the paramedics had Katherine and the baby strapped safely inside on a built-in bed, Lonnie climbed into the back and took a seat out of the way.

The drive to the hospital was rough and slippery, but they managed to make the trip in just over thirty minutes. The medical assistants unloaded the two patients at the emergency doors, where several nurses immediately took charge.

In a matter of moments the women had Katherine and baby pushed into a small examination room, and Lonnie was left outside in the tiled corridor to wait.

Fifteen minutes later he spotted a doctor somewhere near his own age, hurrying down the hallway. A clipboard was jammed under one arm and a stethoscope flopped against his white coat. With a cursory glance at Lonnie, he went into the examining room and shut the door behind him.

Lonnie took his hat off and leaned up against the wall to wait.

For the next thirty minutes a number of things ran through his weary mind. He thought about Seth and the Ketchum family, and how they were going to react to hearing they had another new relative. And more particularly, he kept thinking about himself and his own reaction to the events that had unfolded tonight. Helping Katherine give birth had left him feeling elated, as if he was walking on gold-lined clouds. And now as he waited for the doctor to finish his business, Lonnie was impatient to know that she and the boy were healthy. He wanted to see them again. He wanted the time to pass quickly so that he could take them home and enjoy having them all to himself.

Dear Lord, what had come over him, he wondered. He was thinking and behaving like a husband and a father. That couldn't be. It just couldn't be.

He was mulling over that stunning idea when the examining room door swung open and the doctor emerged. Lonnie pushed himself away from the wall as the man walked straight over to him.

"Sheriff Corteen. I'm Dr. Evan Braden." He reached for Lonnie's hand and shook it firmly. "I understand you delivered Ms. McBride's baby."

Lonnie was suddenly so anxious he had to remind himself to breathe. "That's right. Is everything all right? She had some bleeding—"

"She's fine. Just a little tearing. I've put in some stitches and she'll be sore for a few days, but it's nothing serious. Everything else looks fine. You did a good job."

"And the baby?"

"He's appears to be perfectly healthy. I've clamped his cord and put drops in his eyes—all the things we do for a newborn."

Lonnie gave a long sigh of relief. "I was worried. She wasn't due for a while and—"

Dr. Braden interrupted with a shake of his head. "Due dates aren't etched in stone. Sometimes they can be way off. And in this case I think it was. The baby is full-term. In fact, it's a good thing she went into labor when she did. Another week or two and she might have been forced to have a C-section."

Lonnie was glad about that. Yet he still felt guilty he'd caused her to go through such trauma without any medical help. "So when can I take them home, Doctor?"

The doctor didn't seem to find it odd that a new single mother would be staying with Deaf Smith County's bachelor sheriff. But then, Lonnie supposed this man saw all kinds of situations during a day's work. It would probably be hard to shock him.

Dr. Braden glanced at his wristwatch. "Well, since it's only a few hours until daylight, there's not much sense in your leaving now. Let the nurses keep an eye on them until morning and then they can go."

Lonnie was surprised. "That soon?"

A wry smile crossed the doctor's face. "Sure. She's young and healthy and so is the baby. There's no need to keep them here any longer than that. Especially when I know you're going to take good care of them."

Lonnie felt his cheeks redden. He wasn't the only one who thought he was behaving like a husband and a father. The good doctor thought so, too. Thank goodness none of his deputies were around to see this. He'd never hear the end of it.

"Thanks, Doctor. I will."

Minutes later Katherine and the baby were taken to a private room. Lonnie made an appearance long enough to urge her to rest and to reassure her that he'd be back in a few hours to pick up her and the baby. After that, he found himself a couch in the empty waiting room and was asleep as soon as his head hit the back of the cushion.

Later that morning, Lonnie discovered checking out of a hospital took much longer than checking in. Hours passed before Katherine and the baby were finally signed out and the three of them drove away from the hospital parking lot.

During the night, the storm had moved eastward and the skies had cleared. The weak, wintry sun now glistened over the snow-covered grounds and various long icicles hung from the eaves of buildings all throughout town.

Since Lonnie had ridden into Hereford in the ambulance with Katherine, he'd caught a ride over to the sheriff's office and picked up the SUV he always drove while on duty. Chains had already been attached to the tires, and the small but sturdy vehicle was handling the slippery roads far better than his truck had last night. Even so, he was glad to see the town traffic was still practically nil and that people were using common sense and staying off the roadways.

"You're going to need some things for yourself and the baby before we leave town," he said as he carefully negotiated the vehicle over the snow-packed ice. "If you could make a list, I'll run through the discount store and gather up the stuff while you stay in the vehicle with the baby."

"All right."

She didn't say more, and Lonnie glanced over to see she was staring out the window. A faint frown puckered her brow.

"What's wrong?" he asked quickly.

Her head turned slightly in his direction. "Nothing."

Lonnie's experience with women was limited. But he knew enough to know that "nothing" usually meant everything.

"Now that the baby's come are you wishing you were back in Fort Worth?"

The look she turned on him was one of guilt and regret. "Well, sort of," she admitted. "Don't get me wrong, Lonnie, I appreciate all you're doing. But on the other hand, I don't like burdening you like this. You have a job and your own life to deal with. I'm causing you lots of trouble. And I don't like that."

He let out a long, impatient breath. "Look, you're not causing me trouble. I'll get to work soon enough. Now, let's drop the subject completely," he said, then realizing he'd probably sounded a little gruff, he glanced toward her and grinned. "I'd rather talk about other things. Like your little one there. Have you decided what you're going to name him?"

Her features relaxed as she looked down at the tiny baby in her arms. He was swaddled in a blue receiving blanket the hospital had provided and the nurses had attempted to comb his thick thatch of black hair to one side of his head. He was the most precious, beautiful thing that Katherine had ever seen, and her heart swelled with emotional tears each time she looked at him.

"No. I wanted to talk with you about it first."

His brows lifted as he carefully stopped the SUV at a red light. "Me? What do I have to do with your baby's name?"

"Because I want to name him after you. If that's all right," she added quickly.

It was a good thing they were stopped, Lonnie thought. Otherwise, he might have run smack into the vehicle ahead of them. "Oh, no! Lonnie isn't a name you want to pin on your boy. It's, well, it's sorta redneck. He needs something strong and sophisticated."

A faint smile dimpled her cheeks. "I don't know where you ever got such an idea. I think Lonnie is strong and masculine. Just like you."

In the bright glare of the snow, Lonnie knew there wasn't any way he could hide the red color filtering into his cheeks. He wasn't used to a woman giving him a compliment. Especially not such a personal one.

"That's nice of you, Katherine. But I just don't think—"

"What is your middle name?" she interrupted.

"David."

She smiled. "Lonnie David McBride. I'll call him David. Do you mind?"

He tried to speak, but his throat was suddenly so thick he had to swallow before he could get anything out. "Why no. Why would I mind?"

The traffic light changed and though he desperately wanted to look over at her and the baby, he had to keep his focus on the traffic around them.

Katherine shrugged. "Well, you'll probably get married and have a son of your own someday. Your wife might want to name him Lonnie David, Jr., and then she might not like it that my son is running around with your name."

Lonnie's chuckle was self-deprecating and full of disbelief. "Oh, no, Katherine. No—that won't be happening."

She frowned at him. "How can you sound so sure? Have you sworn off marriage or something?"

Nervously he rubbed a palm against the side of his

face. "Uh, not exactly. But—just believe me when I say I'd be honored for you to name the boy Lonnie David. Real honored."

Several minutes later Lonnie was holding Katherine's long list in one hand and pushing a shopping cart between rows of baby products. Quickly, without too much attention to name brands, he tossed in a car seat, blankets, T-shirts, socks, powder, baby oil, cotton swabs, wet wipes and a bottle. Along with those items, he added a little stuffed horse and a tiny orange cap with the words I'm a Longhorn written above the bill. Now all he needed was to pick up the diapers.

"Well, Sheriff Corteen! What are you doing here?"

Lonnie groaned inwardly as he recognized the voice of one of his closest neighbors. Effie Boatright was a good woman. She worked hard at raising her three grandchildren, whose parents had been killed in a small, commuter plane crash. And Lonnie admired her dogged spirit, but she'd always been on the nosy side, especially where Lonnie's personal life was concerned. Effie hated the idea that he lived alone, and she was always trying to fix him up with a date. Probably because she was lonely, he figured, and she thought that he was lonely, too.

"I have a guest who's just had a baby and she needs a few things."

The large, rawboned woman gave him a bright smile. "Well now, that's excitin'—a guest with a new baby. She from around here?"

Lonnie glanced pointedly at the list and hoped Effie would get the message that he was in a hurry.

"No. From Fort Worth."

"Guess you must be friends with the father."

"Er—something like that." Lonnie never did take to lying about anything. But he knew if he gave Effie a hint of Katherine's situation, she'd have the news spread all over Hereford in a matter of minutes. Not that he was embarrassed about having a woman and a newborn baby in his house. But he didn't want any sort of false rumors to hurt Katherine. She'd already been hurt enough by the man who'd left her.

"Nice seeing you, Effie. You drive safe on these roads," he told the older woman before he hurriedly pushed his cart on down the aisle toward the diapers.

Out in the parking lot, he'd left the engine running in the SUV so the heater would keep Katherine and the baby warm. When he opened the door to load the packages, the sound of little David's squalls blasted his ears.

"What's wrong with him?"

Katherine rocked the baby to and fro in an effort to calm him. "He's hungry."

Lonnie shut the door on the last of the packages and climbed into the driver's seat. He glanced with concern at his new namesake.

"Well, I don't know how you're going to feed the little tot," he exclaimed. "You only had one bottle written down on the list and you didn't have formula written down at all."

Katherine looked at him in amazement and then lifted a hand to her mouth as she started to giggle. "Oh, Lonnie. I'm going to feed him the natural way. We women are equipped for that, you know."

Lonnie's lips parted, and then his face grew ruddy

with embarrassment. "See. I told you I wasn't father material."

She reached over and touched his arm. "I'm not sure I'm mother material, either. I don't guess anyone knows what kind of parent they'll be until they're given the role."

"Maybe. But I should have been using some common sense." He started to put the gearshift into Reverse and then suddenly remembered the car seat he'd purchased. From the looks of the contraption, he figured it would take hours to get the seat strapped securely into place.

He looked over at her and little David, who was still emitting short, angry cries. "I got the car seat," he told her. "But it's too cold to try to set it up now. I'll drive carefully on the way home to the ranch. And if you want—go ahead and feed him. I won't look."

"Thank you, Lonnie."

He backed out of the parking slot and headed the vehicle toward the highway leading out of town. Beside him, he could hear the rustle of Katherine's clothing and then the hungry smack of the baby's lips as it latched on to her nipple.

The image burned Lonnie's mind with all sorts of intimate thoughts, and suddenly he wished that he had the right to watch her nurse the baby, the right to touch her breasts and the rest of her soft body. But she didn't belong to him, and he'd be a fool to think she ever would.

Chapter Eight

Later that afternoon, at the sheriff's office in Hereford, Lonnie held the phone away from his ear as Seth practically shouted at him.

"She had the baby? At your house?"

"That's right," Lonnie told him. "There wasn't anything I could do about it. All the ambulances were tied up, and there wasn't a chance in hell I could have driven her to the hospital. We were barely able to drive to the ranch. So I delivered the baby myself."

Seth made a noise that implied he found the whole incident incredulous. "You know, I've been a lawman for nearly twenty years, and I've never delivered a baby. But you—this is your second one, isn't it? What do you do to women anyway, Lonnie, to get their motors running?"

Still feeling pretty proud of himself, Lonnie grinned.

"I don't know. I guess you could say I've been in the wrong place at the right time or maybe that's the right place at the wrong time. Anyway, I'm beginning to ask myself if I should have been an obstetrician instead of a sheriff. Might be a safer job."

"Dealing with irritable women?" Seth asked with comic disbelief, then turned a more serious question on him. "Where are you now, Lonnie, still at the ranch?"

"No. I'm here at work. At my office."

"Oh. So you got Katherine and the baby to the hospital. I guess they're still there?"

"They spent a few hours there so the doctor could check them out. But they're home now. At the ranch. The doctor didn't see any need to keep them at the hospital." Lonnie smiled, feeling a touch of pride. "She's not wimpy, Seth. I guess you'd say she was a real Ketchum—strong as a whip."

His friend totally ignored the strong part and instead gasped with amazement. "Mother and baby are out at your place? Damn it, Lonnie, they shouldn't be alone!"

Lonnie doodled on a message pad lying among the papers and communication devices scattered across his desk. "I am the sheriff here, Seth. I have responsibilities I need to attend to. Katherine assured me she would be fine for a couple of hours. In fact, I think she was looking forward to having a bit of privacy. You know me—I've probably been smothering her a little too much."

Seth grunted with wry amusement. "Yeah, I imagine you have been smothering her. I guess you two have gotten pretty close during all of this," he added thoughtfully.

Lonnie's doodling stopped as he recalled the images

of Katherine straining to have little David. He'd felt her pain and desperately wanted to take it all away. He'd been frantic at the notion she might hemorrhage to death right before his eyes. And then later, when he'd kissed her, he'd felt as if she was the only woman he was ever supposed to kiss, or even want to kiss. Yeah, he was getting close all right, he decided. But he wasn't about to let himself believe it was a two-sided thing.

"A little."

Lonnie's evasive reply left Seth quiet for a few moments, then he said, "I really think I should come on up there, Lonnie. You can't handle this by yourself. And once I'm there—"

"No!" Lonnie interrupted. "Katherine isn't ready for that. Too much has happened. We haven't even had a chance to discuss you Ketchums yet."

"You were cooped up in your truck for hours yesterday. What did you talk about, the weather?"

"Well, as a matter of fact, it did come up. We were in an ice storm, you know."

Seth groaned and Lonnie grimaced.

"Look, Lonnie, it's like you said a few minutes ago, you have your job to do. Katherine and the baby need care. If you don't want me around, Corrina would be more than happy to drive up and help her."

Corrina was Seth's new wife and a lovely woman. She and Katherine would no doubt get along. But Corrina was a Ketchum. Lonnie didn't want to push anything or anyone about the family on Katherine until she showed him a sign that she was ready.

"I'm sure Corrina would be a big help. But what would I say when she got here? Katherine, your sister-in-law, has come to the ranch to take care of you? Hell, Seth, she hasn't even come to terms with the fact that Celia might not be her real mother."

Seth groaned with frustration. "Then what has all this gained us, Lonnie? You got her to your ranch, but if we can't come see her—"

"Give me time, Seth. I'll nudge her around to seeing y'all. But I want her to feel comfortable about it."

The Texas Ranger on the other end of the line went quiet for long moments, and Lonnie realized this whole thing was hard on his friend. Seth and his family had loved their mother dearly and they'd been through a horrible ordeal with Noah's murder. The Ketchums probably figured that bringing Katherine and her baby into the family would make up for some of the grief they'd dealt with over the past few months.

"You're right, Lonnie. I'm just getting anxious, and now that the baby has come I know everyone in the family is going to be excited to see him."

A broad smile lit Lonnie's face. "Seven pounds and six ounces. Twenty inches long. He looks just like Katherine, Seth. And you're gonna be surprised when you see her. She resembles Victoria a whole lot. She has your mother's dark hair and green eyes."

A faint knock on the office door had Lonnie lifting his head to see one of his deputies entering the room with a fistful of papers. He made a motion to the man to wait, then to Seth he said, "I gotta go, buddy. Work is calling. I'll keep you informed on how things are going out at the ranch."

"All right. But before you go, Lonnie, what did Katherine name her son?"

Thankfully the deputy was studying the notes in his

hand and missed the inanely proud grin he knew was on his face. "Lonnie David."

"That's your name!"

"Yeah, it sure is."

He hung up the phone before Seth could say anything else. Across the desk, the deputy said, "Sorry to interrupt you, Sheriff, but if you've got a minute, could you take a look at this information? I think we need to get the judge to sign a search warrant."

Lonnie took the papers and motioned for the deputy to take a seat. For now, he had to get Katherine and the baby out of his mind, but the sweet knowledge that he'd get to go home to them later made the sun shining across his desk seem a whole lot brighter.

For the next three days, Katherine steadily regained her strength. At the same time baby David was forming a routine of when he wanted to eat and sleep. The weather turned nice and quickly melted away the last vestiges of ice and snow left over from the storm.

Lonnie's house was small, with odds and ends and pieces of furniture that were more comfortable than stylish. As soon as Katherine had been able to walk around and mosey through the rooms, she'd instantly fallen in love with the hominess of the place. Especially the kitchen, which was filled with old dishes and pots and pans that could actually be cooked in rather than just looked at.

This evening she'd found a chicken in the freezer and a bag of noodles in the cupboards, along with a small package of corn bread mix. When Lonnie arrived home from work, he discovered her at the gas range, stirring something in a big pot. The smell of chicken and spices filled the little kitchen, and he sniffed appreciatively.

"I don't know what you're doing, up and cooking, but it sure does smell good in here."

Turning away from the range, she smiled at him. "You'd better wait until you taste it before you compliment me. You didn't exactly have the required spices for chicken soup, but I used what I could find. Don't you ever buy groceries?"

He pulled off his Stetson and hung it on a peg by the door. As he ran a hand through his flattened hair, he said, "Every once in a while I'll go to the store and buy a load of groceries and promise myself I'm going to cook nutritious things to eat rather than grabbing hamburgers or barbecue. But then I get busy and all my good intentions go down the drain."

She watched him pull the sheriff's badge from the left side of his white shirt, then unbuckle the pistol from his hips. After he placed the weapon atop the tall refrigerator, he went over to the table where baby David was sleeping peacefully in a bassinet the two of them had concocted from a rattan basket.

Bending over the basket, Lonnie gently adjusted the blue blanket across the baby's shoulders, then ran a finger over the fine dark hair that Katherine had oiled and brushed to one side.

"He's really something, isn't he?" he whispered.

The tender awe in Lonnie's voice touched Katherine in a deep, emotional way. Just as it always did when she watched his loving reaction to her son. His genuine affection for David made her wish she had met a man like him before Walt. It was also a poignant reminder that her son wouldn't have a father. Especially a father as fine as Lonnie would be.

"I still want to cry with joy when I look at him," she admitted.

Lonnie moved away from the baby and came to stand next to Katherine. As he peered curiously into the bubbling pot, she glanced up at him and felt her heart leap in a happy little jig. Each evening when he came home, she was reminded all over again of his big, strong body and his rugged, manly features. And each time she realized how glad she was to have his company. Living with him like this had turned out to be much sweeter than she'd imagined and she couldn't hide the pleasure she felt whenever he was near.

"How are you feeling?" he asked quietly.

"I'm feeling great. David has been asleep most of the day and I managed to get plenty of rest."

His eyes slipped over her lightly made up face and further down to the thin beige sweater she was wearing over a pair of black slacks. Her full breasts were straining the fabric and her stomach was still a little pudgy, but to Lonnie that only made her sexier and more womanly. There'd been so many times these past three days that he'd found himself wanting to reach out and touch her, to press her soft body next to his. And standing beside her now, he realized the wanting was only getting stronger.

"That's good. But I hope you're not doing this cooking on my account. I don't expect it."

Katherine had to smile. Lonnie was the most undemanding man she'd ever met. That made it even nicer to do something for him.

"I know you don't expect it. It's just something I want to do. And it's nice to have time away from work to cook and do things I don't normally get a chance to."

He remained thoughtfully quiet for a few moments before he asked, "So you're not missing Fort Worth yet?"

These past few days Katherine hadn't really asked herself that question. She'd been too absorbed with her new baby and with getting to know Lonnie and the home he was so generously sharing with her. But now that he'd posed the question, she realized she'd be happy if she never had to see Fort Worth again, which was a scary thought. Her job, her life was there. This time with Lonnie was only a temporary thing.

"Not really. I love the solitude here. And my job can get awfully hectic at times. I'm not quite ready to jump back into it just yet. But don't worry, I'll get out of your hair soon."

He frowned at her. "You're not causing any problems. You can stay as long as you like."

Feeling suddenly awkward, Katherine picked up a spoon and stirred the chicken and noodles. "That's kind of you, Lonnie. But I will have to get back soon."

Just hearing her talk about leaving made him feel empty, and he wondered just how awful this place would be once she did leave. He wished he didn't have to think about it. Now or ever.

"How soon?"

She shrugged and hoped he didn't notice how rapidly her heart was beating beneath her sweater. "Oh, I don't know. Before long."

He didn't speak for a minute or two and when he did,

his voice was low and husky. "Katherine, is there someone back in Fort Worth that you're…close to?"

Her head twisted around and she looked up at him
in surprise. "Close to? You mean, like a boyfriend?"

He nodded solemnly. "Yeah, like a boyfriend or a—
lover."

It was all she could do not to wince at the last word.
For months now whenever she'd thought of Walt, she'd
vowed she would never let another man make love to
her. But since Lonnie had appeared at her apartment,
she'd been having long, second thoughts about that vow
of celibacy.

"No! Not at all," she said flatly, and with a deep
breath she went back to her stirring.

Sensing her agitation, he placed his hands gently
around her shoulders. It was all Katherine could do not
to lean her head back against his chest, to sigh and simply let his warm strength fill her with pleasure.

"Are you sure?"

"Positive. Why do you ask, anyway?"

Because he was becoming obsessed with her, Lonnie thought. Because he couldn't bear to think of another man doing the things that he'd been doing these
past days for Katherine and baby David.

Aloud, he said, "I just wonder about you and David
once you get back to Fort Worth. You're a lovely
woman, Katherine. I'm sure there's going to be plenty
of men flocking around you."

Closing her eyes, she bit down on her lip. "No.
You're wrong, Lonnie. Not too many young men want
to take on a ready-made family."

I would. The two words popped into his head so

quickly he almost blurted them out to her. Thank God he'd caught himself in time. Since the baby's birth, he'd felt a closeness growing between them. He didn't want to say anything that might tear that friendly bond apart.

"You might be surprised," he murmured. "There are plenty of men who'd be proud to be David's father."

Katherine stared at a spot on the range as Richard Marek came to mind. Several times he'd hinted to Katherine that he'd be more than happy to be a father to her baby. On top of that, Althea had urged her to go after the man. But Katherine hadn't wanted Richard in any way, shape or form, and she wanted him even less now.

"Well, I do know one," she admitted. "But I'm not interested in him."

Jealousy stabbed Lonnie deep, but he told himself he had to be sensible. Katherine was a young, beautiful woman. She was going to need and want a man in her life. The least he could do was urge her to weed out the bad ones and hang on to a good one.

"Why not?"

She sighed. "For one thing, he's my boss."

Lonnie was so surprised by her admission that his hands slipped from her shoulders. "Your boss," he repeated slowly. "You mean—the tax assessor himself?"

The incredulous tone of his voice caused Katherine's lips to form a grim line. It probably sounded scandalous to Lonnie, she thought. A young, pregnant woman playing around with an elected official, and on county time to boot. But it hadn't been that way. Nor would it ever be that way.

"That's him," she conceded.

"Oh."

"Yeah, oh," she said glumly. "Lately he's been making my job really difficult. He's made it pretty clear he wants to—share a life with me. I've tried to be clear with him that I'm not interested. But some men don't seem to want to take no for an answer."

Turning away from her, Lonnie jammed his hands in his pockets and walked back over to little David. Just the sight of the baby's face filled him with an overwhelming need to protect him. Maybe this tax assessor would be a wonderful father to David. But what if he wasn't? This little guy might grow up unloved and unwanted, and Lonnie couldn't bear that thought.

"Well, he must be a good man," Lonnie said, trying his best to be fair. "And in his position he could make a good home for you. Maybe you should give the guy a chance."

Whirling around, Katherine glowered at him. "Let me tell you, I don't need Richard Marek to make a home for me. I'm not helpless, I can make my own home!"

Seeing he'd stirred her ire, Lonnie held up both hands. "Sorry. I didn't realize the male gender was such a sticky subject with you."

The anger on her face disappeared, only to be replaced by awkward confusion.

"It's—they're not a sticky subject," she countered. "I just don't like the idea of you trying to marry me off to someone. How would you like it if I told you that you needed to marry someone because she was a good woman? Because she would make you a good home?"

Put like that, it sounded so ridiculous that Lonnie had to grin. "I guess I wouldn't like it. I have my own ideas about who I'd marry."

She heaved out a pent-up breath. Dear Lord, the man didn't know just how sexy he was, Katherine thought. He didn't have a clue as to how he made her heart race, her body stir with longing. And that was probably for the best. It would only put him in an uncomfortable position if he knew how much his houseguest was attracted to him.

"So do I," she murmured. "So lets talk about something else, okay?"

He made a careful study of her face before he finally said, "Sure. How long till supper? I need to do my feeding down at the barn."

Even though she'd not been able to get out of the house these past three days to look around the ranch, she'd learned that Lonnie owned several head of horses and a modest herd of Hereford cattle. During the winter months, the pastures were dormant and the animals required feed and hay on a daily basis. Taking care of the livestock was the first thing Lonnie attended to in the evenings before he settled in for supper.

"Thirty minutes. But don't hurry, I'll keep it warm for you," she told him.

His expression a little sheepish, he walked back over to where she stood and placed a hand on her shoulder. Katherine relished the closeness of his touch, the warmth in his eyes as his gaze caressed her face.

"I'm sorry if I offended you, Katherine. I just want you and David to be happy, that's all."

Lonnie made her happy. With each passing day she was realizing that more and more. Yet he hadn't made any suggestion, not even a hint he was interested in having a relationship with her. Now he'd implied that

her boss could give her a good home! That ought to be
more than enough to tell her he wasn't attracted to her
in a romantic way.

"By marrying me off?" she asked, trying to hide the
weary frustration she was suddenly feeling.

Lonnie's eyes slipped to the toes of his boots. At the
same time his hand slid from her shoulder. "I guess all
women don't want to be married. I really don't know
how I could have forgotten that."

He sounded bitter, almost to the point of being sharp,
and Katherine suddenly realized she was seeing a side
of this man that he kept mostly hidden.

"What is that supposed to mean?"

"Nothing."

"Lonnie…what—"

With a shake of his head, he interrupted, "Forget it,
Katherine. I've got…things to do."

For one second, as he turned away from her, Katherine almost reached out and grabbed his arm to stop
him. But something held her back. Instead, she watched
him slap his hat back on his head and step out the door.
A few moments passed before she heard him crossing
the porch, and she knew he'd paused long enough to
shrug on the old work jacket he'd left hanging on a
nearby peg.

When the sound of his footsteps finally faded away,
she turned back to her cooking and firmly told herself
that she didn't need to know the inner workings of Lonnie Corteen. If he'd had woman problems in his past, that
was none of her business. Still, Katherine didn't want to
think that some woman had hurt him. He was too good,
too precious, to be treated unkindly by the opposite sex.

Chapter Nine

Two hours later Katherine sat curled up on the couch in the living room, in front of the crackling fire Lonnie had built in the fireplace. While he cleaned the kitchen, the heat from the flames was working wonders to relax her muscles. She stared drowsily at the glowing embers while, a couple of cushions away, David slept peacefully in his basket.

"Surely I don't have to tell you that you can turn on the television anytime you like. I don't watch it much, but you're welcome to help yourself."

She glanced around to see Lonnie bringing in two steaming cups of coffee. He brought the drinks over to the coffee table and sat down between Katherine and the baby.

"I hope you don't mind me wedging in between you two," he said. "I like sitting here in front of the fire."

"I don't mind at all," she murmured as she took the

nearest mug. "It was very nice of you to build it for me. Especially when I know firewood is a scarce commodity out here on the plains."

After Lonnie was settled between her and the baby, his long legs stretched comfortably out in front of him, he said, "I usually go back to East Texas each fall to do some hunting with an old friend. He lets me cut all the firewood I want on his place. So I pull a flatbed trailer and load it and the truck with wood before I head home."

"I've never lived in a house with a fireplace," Katherine admitted. Then with a contented sigh she said, "It sure makes the room warm and inviting. And I like it quiet—like now—without the television. You can hear the flames crackling and the wind blowing. That's much nicer than car horns, squealing tires and revving motors."

Lonnie took a careful sip from his coffee mug as he watched the glow of the firelight flicker over her lovely profile. She seemed to enjoy being here on the ranch, and he could tell she'd taken to the solitude like a duck to water. Yet she'd only been here a few days, he told himself. A few more and the place might begin to grate on her nerves.

"You know, several times you've mentioned the quietness out here on the Rafter C. It makes me wonder why you ever moved to Fort Worth in the first place," he mused aloud. "Why didn't you stay around Canyon or move back here to Hereford. This is where you and Celia originally lived, isn't it?"

Cradling her mug with both hands, Katherine shrugged. "Yes, we lived there when I was a baby. Then, by the time I was in elementary school, Mother decided, for some reason, to move us up to Canyon," she said thoughtfully. "As for me living in Fort Worth, well, with Mother gone, I knew it all depended on me to keep things going monetarily. You see, right before she died, when she became very ill, I had to quit the part-time job I had between college classes in order to take care of her. And her medical bills pretty much depleted the money we'd saved between us. I desperately needed a good job and I figured it would be easier to find one in Fort Worth. And I...I guess I hoped that a large city would make me not think of Mother so much. She was the only person I had and it's pretty tough to be out in the world all alone."

Lonnie studied the brown liquid in his cup. "Katherine, you've had a lot to think about the past few days and I—" He stopped as the baby began to squirm and emit a fussy cry.

Quickly Katherine rose to her feet, and Lonnie pulled his legs up and out of her path as she moved to the end of the couch and peered into the makeshift bassinet.

"Hello, my little darling," she crooned to the baby. "Are you hungry again?"

Little David's arms flailed the air as his face turned the color of a ripe tomato. Katherine gently lifted him out of the basket and placed him on the cushion next to Lonnie.

"I'm not necessarily trying to run you off, but you might want to get up and move to another part of the room," she suggested. "I'm going to change his diaper and I'm pretty certain it's really dirty."

Lonnie didn't have to be told twice. He bolted from the couch and went to stand by the fireplace. Turning his back to the flames, he asked, "Can I get you something? Diapers? Wipes?"

Reaching beneath the coffee table, she pulled out a little box that she appeared to be using as a makeshift diaper bag. The squared cardboard was crammed with disposable diapers, powder, oil, wipes, all the things needed to care for a baby's hygiene. Lonnie made a mental note to go by the store and buy her a regular diaper bag. The box served the purpose, but she could hardly carry it out anywhere.

"Thanks," she said, "but I have it all right here."

She cleaned and diapered the baby with gentle thoroughness, then bundled him back in a thin blue blanket. Once she was finished, she carried him over to the rocker and momentarily turned to one side as she fumbled with her clothing.

With her back still turned to Lonnie, she mumbled, "This will be much easier when I finally get some nursing bras. I hope I can get to a store soon. There are so many things I need."

"You should have told me sooner that you needed to go to the store. Whenever you think you're up to it, I'll drive you into town."

Finally she straightened back around in the rocker and Lonnie saw that the baby and part of her breast were covered with a receiving blanket. The other part, a hint of white flesh just above the blanket, was exposed to his eye, and it was all Lonnie could do to keep from staring at the exquisite mound of flesh.

"If the weather holds fair maybe we could go tomorrow or the next day," she suggested. "But I don't want to interfere with your work. I could drive your old ranch truck and then you wouldn't have to bother."

Lonnie frowned at her. "You can't drive a vehicle this soon. And it's no bother for me to take you. As long as there's not an emergency going on, I can make my own hours. It's not like Hereford is a huge metropolis that needs my constant attention."

Katherine supposed he could make his own hours, but still she felt guilty. She glanced at Lonnie as she pushed the chair into a gentle sway. "I believe you were about to ask me something before David interrupted. What was it?"

She had beautiful skin, he thought. Beautiful and soft. When she'd been in labor, he'd touched her thighs and belly and, even though he'd not done it in a sexual way, he could still remember how silky and smooth she'd felt. No doubt her breast would be just as silky and just as warm and luscious as her lips had been.

"Lonnie?" she repeated when he failed to answer. "What was it that you were going to ask me?"

Mentally shaking himself, he directed his gaze to a safe spot at the other side of the room. "Nothing really. I…well, it is something, too," he corrected. "I've been thinking about you and the Ketchums. You haven't asked about them. Not once since you've been here."

Katherine's gaze dropped to the tiny boy cradled in her arms. It scared her to think of the Ketchums. The thought that her own mother, the only relative she'd had in the world, might not have been her mother at all, was so devastating her mind refused to ponder the notion for more than a minute at a time.

"I've had other things on my mind. It isn't every day that a woman becomes a mother for the first time."

"No," he said with slow deliberation. "I realize you've been occupied. But I think you ought to know that Seth and his family are real excited about the little one, there. They'd all like to see him."

Surprised at this news, she looked up at him. "You've told them about David being born?"

Lonnie nodded. "I guess I'm just a little too proud of him. I can't keep quiet."

"Too bad his father hadn't felt that way. Proud, I mean." Her gaze moved down from Lonnie's face to the flickering flames of the fire. "But he wasn't proud that I was going to have his child. Far from it, in fact." She paused, sighed softly, then went on in a quiet voice. "I made such a bad judgment with Walt. It makes me feel like a fool now. And very guilty. A woman is supposed to sense those sorts of things in a man—whether he'd be a good husband and a good father. I realized he was young like me and he had some growing up to do, but I really believed he cared about me. Now my son is going to suffer because I didn't see his father for what he really was."

The self-blame he heard in her voice was achingly familiar to Lonnie, and in that moment all he wanted to do was take it all away from her.

Groaning softly, he went over to the rocker and knelt to one side of her knees. Then with one hand on each arm of the chair, he leaned toward her. "Katherine, you shouldn't feel guilty. I'm sure Walt purposely deceived you into thinking he was serious. That's the way some men work. And some women. Believe me, I know."

Her eyes widened with faint surprise, and for long moments she studied his rugged face, searched the depths of his blue eyes for the secrets he'd hidden inside.

"Lonnie, earlier when you said something about some woman not wanting to marry, were you talking about someone you were once close to?"

Lonnie pursed his lips. He didn't want to admit to Katherine that he'd made such a mistake with Ginger. He didn't want her to know he'd been that hungry for companionship or so naive where women were concerned. But Katherine had been open with him about her misfortune with David's father. And maybe telling her about the humiliation he'd been through would help her. After all, that was what he wanted the most—to ease this woman's heart.

Clearing his throat, he glanced away from her and focused his gaze on the shadows across the room. "Yes. There was a woman once. A few years ago. I trusted her to always be there for me, but in the end she let me down."

"Did you love her?"

Had he? At one time Lonnie had been besotted with the long-legged blonde. All he'd been able to think about was the two of them being together. But that was then. Now as he turned his gaze back to Katherine's lovely face, he realized the things he'd felt for Ginger had been shallow compared to the emotions Katherine elicited in him.

"No. Oh, at the time I believed it was love. But I was young and lonely and my body was begging for a mate. If you know what I mean," he added wryly.

Disbelief crossed her face. "You lonely? I can't believe that, Lonnie. I'm sure you've never had trouble getting women to date you."

His eyes lifted to the ceiling as a humorless chuckle

slipped from his throat. "Oh, Katherine, you are good for a man's ego."

She frowned at him. "I didn't say that to stroke your ego, Lonnie. I meant it. You're a strong, nice-looking guy. You have an admirable job and on top of that you're sweet. Women don't usually run from men like you."

His eyes left the ceiling to connect with hers. "Humph. You haven't always known me, Katherine."

"I know you now."

A long breath pushed past his lips as he rose to his feet and walked back over to the fireplace. "Do you want to know why I really made such a bad mistake with Ginger?" he asked with faint bitterness. "It was because— well, I wasn't just lonely, I was hungry. Hungry for any kind of attention from the opposite sex. I haven't always looked like I do now, Katherine. Growing up, I was tall and skinny. My feet were too big for the rest of my body, and I would often get tangled up and trip over myself. My hair was bright copper and I had a faceful of freckles to match. In high school, girls didn't look at me and if they did, it was to tease me. And with my parents dead and gone, I didn't have anyone around to tell me I was worthy or wanted. I grew up thinking I was ugly and that no female would ever have anything to do with me. So when Ginger cruised into Carrizozo and settled her pretty gaze right on me, I was wildly flattered, to say the least."

"How old were you then?"

"Oh, maybe twenty-three. I was starting to change a little then. My body had filled out—the freckles had faded, along with the brightness of my hair. Ginger's attention was a balm to my ego and I ate it up. I thought it was love. I thought she wanted to marry me."

As Katherine studied his downcast face, her heart squeezed with pain for him. In her wildest dreams she couldn't imagine this strong, handsome man ever having such low self-esteem. She couldn't imagine a woman teasing him, deceiving him. It was unbelievable.

"You obviously broke up," Katherine stated. "So what happened? Why did she even come to your town, anyway?"

He grimaced. "She was a student at New Mexico State University, off for summer vacation. She'd come to Carrizozo to visit relatives and I guess the little desert town was boring to her after the hustle and bustle of college at Las Cruces. She needed something to entertain her and that something was me. But by summer's end she was finished playing with me. She went back to Las Cruces to complete her education. But not before she laughed in my face and told me that she'd never marry a bumpkin like me."

"Oh, Lonnie," she said in a stricken voice. "I'm so sorry."

A mocking, guttural sound erupted from him. "Don't be sorry. Ginger was far from wife material. It just took me a while to understand that."

Little David had stopped nursing. Katherine peeped beneath the blanket to see the baby was sound asleep so she smoothed her clothing over her breast and carried him to the couch.

After she'd carefully positioned her son on his back in the rattan basket, she tucked a heavier blanket around his shoulders, then placed a tiny kiss on his forehead.

Across the way, Lonnie watched her movements and

ached with a need he'd never felt before. It wasn't just the fact that he wanted this woman in his bed. God help him, he wanted her in his life. He wanted to come home to her every day and every night. He wanted to see his own children in her arms.

Rising up from the basket, Katherine walked over to the fireplace and stood close to Lonnie's side. He looked down at her, his brows arched.

Placing her hand on his arm, she gave him a crooked smile, "You know what I say about your Ginger?"

"No," he answered a little warily. "And I'm almost afraid to ask."

She chuckled softly and Lonnie was reminded again of how much he liked to hear her laugh, to see her smile. She was meant to be happy. He wanted her to be happy, even more than he wanted it for himself.

"I say good riddance. You didn't need someone like her."

This woman understood what he'd gone through far more than he'd expected her to, and suddenly he felt as if he'd shed an old skin pitted with deep scars.

"After a while I could see that I was better off without her, Katherine. But, do you have any idea how humiliating it is to a man to have a woman reject him, put him down as though he was nothing more than a pastime?"

Her fingers slid gently, sweetly up his arm and back down again. "I know exactly how humiliating it feels. Walt pretty much put me through the same thing."

Lonnie cupped the side of her face with his big hand. "And I'd pretty much like to knock his head off," he murmured huskily. "I hate like hell that he hurt you, Katherine."

Her heartbeat quickened as she watched his eyes settle on her mouth.

"Lonnie, I—"

The words she'd been about to say suddenly stopped as his eyes darkened and his head dipped toward hers.

"Katherine, don't say anything," he whispered. "Just let me kiss you. That's what I want to do. So much."

Joy splintered inside her and before she had time to consider the consequences of being close to him, she stepped into his arms and raised her mouth to his.

This time when he kissed her she wasn't weary from the aftermath of childbirth. This time she was thinking only of him and the iron-hard band of his arms circling her waist, the warmth of his chest pressing against hers and the domination of his lips as he tasted and coaxed.

In only a matter of moments a low moan emitted from somewhere deep inside her and she opened her lips and allowed his tongue to thrust past her teeth.

The intimate contact sent her head reeling and her hands clinging to his back. Heat raced up and down her spine and collected in her loins like a pool of molten lava ready to explode.

Breathing hard, Lonnie eventually lifted his mouth and looked at her. All Katherine could do was look back at him and moan incoherently.

"Katherine—my sweet little Katherine—I guess you can see how much I want you."

There was a wry tone to his voice, as though he already understood that he couldn't have her and she couldn't have him. The thought filled her with such disappointment that tears stung her eyes.

"And I want you, too, Lonnie," she whispered.

"Do you really, Katherine?"

To answer his question, she went up on tiptoe and pressed her lips to his waiting mouth.

Once again his kiss devoured her lips, his hands splayed against the small of her back, then slid upward until he was gripping both of her shoulders. As he urged her body close to his, she could feel her breasts tingling, the nipples tightening into hard buds.

She wanted him to touch her all over, to kiss her, to taste every intimate part of her. The unsolicited thoughts should have shocked her. But they didn't. Everything about being in Lonnie's arms felt right and good. Except that it had to end, her mind tacked on. For the sake of her baby and herself, she had to pull away from him while she still could.

The faint stirring of Katherine's body was enough to tell Lonnie something was wrong. Easing his head up, he sucked in several long breaths of air.

"Did I hurt you? Damn it, Katherine, I'm a lughead. You shouldn't be doing this. You've just had a baby and—"

Placing a finger against his lips, she whispered gently, "We weren't doing anything that could hurt me." Unless you count breaking my heart, she thought sadly.

"I know. But we, uh…" His hands kneaded her shoulders as he searched for the right words. "We might have gotten carried away. Hell, I *was* carried away."

Tenderly she clasped his face with trembling hands, and as she gazed up at him, her heart suddenly swelled with an emotion she didn't quite understand.

"Lonnie, that's not what I'm concerned about. I mean, you're right, it wouldn't be safe for me to…to make love so soon after the baby. But I…"

As her words trailed away, color seeped into her cheeks. Dropping her head, she stared at the stone hearth beneath their feet and wondered how she could explain herself without hurting him.

Sensing her troubled thoughts, his hand closed around her chin and gently lifted her face up to his. "But you don't want us to be kissing. Is that what you're trying to tell me?"

A helpless groan slipped from her throat. "I don't know how to explain, Lonnie. I like kissing you. I like it too much."

He looked perplexed. "I don't understand, Katherine. If you like it, what's the problem? I would never force you to do anything you didn't want to do."

Turning her back to him, she heaved out a heavy sigh. "I never dreamed that you would. I'm just not ready for this. I have so much going on in my life. And I'll be honest, Lonnie, after Walt I'm not in any hurry to get involved with another man."

"You think I could be like him?"

He sounded incredulous, offended and even hurt. Yet Katherine couldn't help it. She'd been betrayed and hurt herself. She just didn't have it in her to trust so easily again.

"No. Clearly, you're nothing like Walt. But—you've had your own problems and I can't see you wanting to take on more with a single mother and infant son."

He moved up behind her and slipped his arms around her waist. When his voice sounded close to her ear, she shivered with longing.

"How do you know I wouldn't want to take on you and David?"

Suddenly she was trembling with fear. She cared for this man. Cared for him deeply. If she allowed herself to fall in love with him, she'd be opening her heart up to all sorts of pain.

"I just do, Lonnie. You've been a bachelor for a long time. That tells me a lot. That you like living alone and that you don't trust women."

She was right about that last part, Lonnie thought. He didn't like the idea of handing his heart over to another woman. Not after Ginger. But damn it, Katherine was different! She made him look at the future and believe that this time he could be happy. This time he could have real love.

With his cheek pressed against hers, he said, "You're wrong, Katherine, I've never liked living alone. But I can't deny the part about not trusting women. That's pretty hard to do when you've been taken for a ride like the one Ginger took me on. But I don't believe you're anything like her. If I did, well, you wouldn't be living here with me—like this."

Slowly she turned in the circle of his arms and, for a moment, as Katherine looked up at his face, it was all she could do to keep from flinging herself against his broad chest and crying out just how much she wanted and needed him.

"I thank you for that much, Lonnie. But I still think…no," she corrected, "I *know* that we should just be friends."

Friends? The word bounced around inside him like a loose marble. How could they be just friends, he wondered wildly. He'd delivered her baby! He'd seen and touched the most intimate parts of her body! He'd kissed her like there was no tomorrow and she'd kissed him back with a fervor that had stolen his breath. They couldn't go back to being friends. Not now. Not ever.

"Maybe that's how you think of things, Katherine. But I'm willing to wait and see."

Chapter Ten

The next day was beautiful. To Katherine, looking out the window of Lonnie's ranch house, the bright-blue sky seemed to stretch forever. Nearby, in the yard, a few gold-and-red leaves still clung to the branches of several cottonwood trees. The snow and ice that had coated the countryside with a layer of white several days ago had quickly melted away to expose yellow winter grass and late-autumn foliage. But even though the remnants of the snow and ice were gone now, the memories of that storm still lingered in Katherine's mind.

She'd been so very frightened, especially for her child. But Lonnie had soothed her fears. He'd touched her with a firm confidence that had assured her, that had made her believe he would never let anything happen to her. There was no doubt she was deeply grateful to him for helping to bring her son safely into the world.

And last night, after Katherine had kissed him so recklessly, she'd tried to tell herself that gratefulness was the reason she'd stepped so willingly into his arms.

But now, in the bright morning light, she had to admit, at least to herself, that she'd been feeling far more than grateful when she'd kissed Lonnie. She'd wanted him with a fervor that, when she thought about it, still warmed her blood. Yet no matter how she felt, she told herself fiercely, she couldn't let it happen again.

She was just one step away from loving him and even though she could see that he was a good man, that didn't mean he was the right one for her. Being a good man didn't mean that he would stick around through thick and thin. After a few days or even weeks, he might grow tired of having her and the baby around. He might decide having a ready-made family wasn't what he wanted after all. And then where would she be?

Katherine didn't want to think about that possibility as she gently washed David's soft skin. She had a baby to think about now and her job back in Fort Worth. She wasn't going to risk her security—or her heart—for any man.

At the kitchen table, with the warm sunlight streaming through the windows, she finished giving David a bath. A task that was turning out to be far more pleasant than yesterday's, when he'd cried at the top of his lungs the whole way through. This morning her son seemed to be enjoying the feel of the warm water cascading over his little body and his vague blue gaze stared curiously up at her as she crooned and talked to him in a quiet voice.

After rubbing him down with lotion, she dressed the boy in a pair of blue sleepers and placed him back in the basket. Just as she was tucking Lonnie's little stuffed horse near the baby's feet, the telephone rang.

Picking up the basket, she carried the baby with her to the living room to answer the call. Several times, during the past few days, Katherine had answered the phone to find an irate resident of the county phoning to complain to Sheriff Corteen about stolen property or trivial threats made by acquaintances or neighbors.

Expecting this call to be similar, she braced herself before she picked up the receiver. "Sheriff Corteen's residence," she answered brightly.

"Hello. Is this Katherine? Katherine McBride?"

The voice was warm and male and not anyone that she recognized. Katherine went on instant alert as her mind whirled, trying to recognize who the caller might be. Could it be one of Lonnie's deputies? Had Lonnie been injured or worse?

Her heart racing with sudden fear, she answered warily. "Yes, I'm Katherine McBride. Is there something I can do for you?"

There was a slight pause and then the caller said, "I hope I'm not disturbing you, and I know Lonnie's going to be as mad as hell when he finds out I called you, but—I just couldn't wait any longer."

Katherine couldn't explain why, but all of a sudden she didn't have to guess who was on the other end of the line. Her hands and knees began to shake, forcing her to take a seat on the arm of the couch.

"You're Seth," she said matter-of-factly, "the Texas Ranger."

The man released a long breath and Katherine realized with amazement that this Texas Ranger was actually nervous about talking to her. Which didn't make a lick of sense. The man didn't have anything to lose. He already had brothers and a sister, money and social standing. None of that would vanish if she decided not to join their family. On the other hand, Katherine was the one who'd be the loser if she allowed these people to draw her into their fold and then have them kick her out for one reason or another.

"That's right. I guess Lonnie has told you about me."

His voice was slow, his words deliberate. Could this really be her brother, Katherine wondered frantically. Just the idea shook her with all sorts of strong emotions.

"Uh, yes—yes, he has," she stuttered.

"How are you making out up there on the Rafter C?" he asked.

Relieved that he wasn't plowing right into the subject of the circumstances of her birth, Katherine released a silent, pent-up breath. "I'm doing fine. Lonnie is a...wonderful guy. He's made sure I have everything I need and that I'm comfortable."

"I have no doubt about that. Lonnie and I have been friends for a long time. There's none better."

"He thinks highly of you, too." She realized she was gripping the telephone so hard that her fingers were starting to ache. She focused her gaze on the rolling plains beyond the nearby window and told herself to relax. This man couldn't hurt her. She wouldn't let him hurt her.

"I heard about you giving birth to your son there on the ranch. You must be a strong woman."

Even if this man wasn't her brother, to receive a compliment like that from a Texas Ranger was certainly enough to put a faint smile on her face. "Thank you. But Lonnie probably thinks otherwise. I'm afraid, he, uh, had to calm me down a few times."

"Believe me, Katherine, Lonnie thinks you're just about the bravest woman that's ever walked this earth. And coming from him, that's saying a lot."

Hot color filled Katherine's cheeks. She struggled for some sort of suitable reply, but everything that came to mind would only make it sound as if she adored Lonnie. And that was the last thing she wanted Seth Ketchum to think. Because he would no doubt share this conversation with his good law buddy.

"Are you—is there anything that you and the baby need?" Seth asked. "Is he doing okay?"

Katherine swallowed at the sincerity she heard in this man's voice. He sounded as though he really cared whether she and the baby were okay or in need. How could that be if he'd never even met her? And how could he be so warm to her if she really was the product of his mother's affair with Noah Rider? The whole notion was beyond Katherine's comprehension. But maybe the Ketchums were a special breed.

"The baby is doing great. And there's nothing we really need. Lonnie has seen to that."

"Thank God for Lonnie, huh?" Seth asked.

She could hear a smile in his voice, yet she understood his humor was filled with fondness not mockery.

"He's wonderful," she said, and in that moment, she realized she couldn't have meant it more. Lonnie was unlike any man she'd ever met.

"I don't suppose you've thought yet about going up to the T Bar K."

He'd said it more as a statement than a question, yet Katherine felt inclined to answer him anyway. The man had taken the time to call her. He deserved that much.

"No. Having my son ahead of time has sort of…changed things."

She could hear him take a deep breath and let it out. Funny how she felt like doing the same thing.

"That's understandable. I just hope you know that if you do decide to go, we're all looking forward to meeting you. And your new little boy, too. My wife and I—Corrina—we're trying to get pregnant. If she gets her hands on your little boy, you'll probably have a time getting him back. She wants another son."

Katherine's eyes drifted over to David. She would love another son, too, she realized. A tall, auburn-haired son with big hands and a slow, easy smile.

"Another son?" she asked.

"Yes," he answered. "When the two of us married, Corrina already had Matthew, a twelve-year-old son. I've adopted him as my own, and now we'd like one or two more to go with him."

A nice family for a nice man, Katherine thought. She was glad for him. Just as she would be glad for anyone. But if he was thinking that *she* could be a part of his family, too, then he was sadly mistaken. Even if Amelia McBride was her true mother, Katherine was still from different stock.

"I wish you luck, Mr. Ketchum."

"Katherine, I realize this is—"

The rest of his words stopped abruptly as a male voice in the background relayed what sounded to Katherine like an urgent message.

"Sorry, Katherine," he said hastily. "An emergency has just come up. Thank you for talking with me. And take care."

"Yes," she said, her throat tight. "Goodbye."

Katherine dropped the receiver back on its hook and then rose to her feet. She felt extremely weak and shaky and she realized the conversation with Seth Ketchum had affected her far more than it should have. And why was that? She'd told Lonnie she didn't believe that incredible story about Amelia McBride being her mother. But days had passed since Lonnie had first appeared at her apartment door, and a lot had happened between that time and now.

Being here on the Rafter C, away from the hustle and bustle of her life in Fort Worth, had given Katherine more time to think. And the more she thought about the whole Ketchum story, the more she believed that Lonnie was not the sort of man who'd go around telling tall tales without some sort of truth to verify it. Nor did she suspect for one minute that Seth Ketchum would lie.

But to believe the two men would mean that Katherine would have to face the fact that Celia McBride had lied to her. That the woman who had mothered her had not really been her mother at all. The whole thing crushed her heart.

Back in Hereford, Lonnie checked his watch then thoughtfully drummed his fingers on his desk. He'd worked through a major amount of paperwork this morning and thankfully there hadn't been any felony crimes committed in the past few days to require his attention. As far as the Sheriff's Department went, things were going smoothly. If he wanted to take an extra hour off for lunch, it wouldn't hurt a thing. Except that he wanted to used that extra time to spend with Katherine.

You're really getting it bad, Corteen. You think about the woman from morning till night. And when you're asleep, you're dreaming about her. What are you going to do when she up and leaves? Heads back to Fort Worth where that job and that boss of hers is waiting?

The little voice shouting in his ear put a tight grimace on Lonnie's face as he leaned up in his chair and spoke into the intercom on his desk. "Mitch, could you come in here for a minute?"

Almost immediately, a young blond deputy dressed in a tan uniform and a brown Stetson walked into the small room Lonnie called an office and stood before his boss's desk.

"You need me, sir?"

Mitch wasn't his chief deputy, but he was one of Lonnie's most trusted men on the force. The tall, lanky guy had a quick wit and an arrogance that sometimes grated on his nerves. But Lonnie considered the man the same as he would a younger brother.

"You have anything going on right now?" Lonnie asked him.

"Filling out the paperwork for a domestic call last night. That's all."

"You think you can keep a watch on things for a couple of hours? I need to make a trip out to the ranch."

The deputy shrugged both shoulders as if to say he could manage the task with both hands tied behind his back. "Sure, Sheriff."

Lonnie nodded his appreciation. "I realize it's your lunchtime and you usually go down to the diner. But once I get back, I'll see that you get your regular hour and then some."

"Thanks, sir. Bernie will appreciate that."

Lonnie's brows lifted in question. "Bernie?"

Mitch grinned. "Yeah, you know, down at the diner. The cute little brunette with freckles on her nose. She's got the hots for me."

His expression wry, Lonnie said, "Oh? Her and how many others?"

Mitch's grin broadened. "I'm really not sure. I haven't been counting here lately."

"No. I don't imagine you have enough fingers and toes for that."

Ignoring Lonnie's jab, Mitch cocked his hat back off his forehead and peered curiously at his boss. "What's the matter? Are you feelin' sick or something? You need to go lay down for a while?"

Folding his arms across his chest, Lonnie gave the deputy a pointed look. "No, I'm *feelin'* fine. I need to…bring Katherine and the baby into town."

Mitch's brows lifted suggestively. "Ohh, this is time off for the houseguest, huh?" Without waiting for Lonnie's reply, he went on with a wicked grin. "You know, I still don't know how you ended up having a female houseguest—or whatever she is. How did you do it, anyway?"

Lonnie's brow puckered into a frown. "Do what?"

"Get a beautiful woman from Fort Worth to follow you all the way out here?"

Rising to his feet, Lonnie crossed the room and plucked his Stetson from a coatrack. "That, my good buddy, is none of your business." He plopped the hat on his head and adjusted the brim on his forehead. "And how the heck do you know that she's beautiful, anyway? Have people been talking?"

Mitch rolled his eyes. "Just about every nurse in the hospital."

Lonnie's grunt was full of humor. "And from the stories I hear, you're acquainted with plenty of nurses, along with waitresses."

"A man needs to be prepared for all sorts of emergencies."

Lonnie pulled on a heavy jacket. "Well, hopefully none of those 'emergencies' will come up while I'm gone," he said dryly.

The young deputy straightened his shoulders. "Naw, that's not likely to happen, Sheriff. You go on and don't worry about a thing. You know I'll handle it."

"I never worry when you're in charge, Mitch."

Lonnie started out the door, and the deputy called after him. "Hey, Sheriff. Are you gettin' serious about this woman?"

Lonnie's brow puckered as he glanced back at the deputy. "What do you mean, serious?"

Mitch held up his hands in a way that said he couldn't believe Lonnie was asking such a question. "I'm talking about love! I mean, are you crazy about her?"

Crazy wasn't nearly strong enough for the way Lonnie felt about Katherine. Yet he was going crazy wondering what he was going to do about his feelings. Clearly, she didn't believe she was ready to fall in love. And even if she was, that didn't mean she would fall in love with him. He was a fool to believe he might be able to change her mind. But Lonnie had to try. Otherwise, his heart was going to break.

"Yeah, Mitch. I'm afraid I am crazy about the woman."

On his way to the ranch, Lonnie used his cell phone to call Katherine and alert her to be ready to make a trip into town. She'd assured him that she'd be waiting, but Lonnie had detected a strained note in her voice. Rather than question her about it over the phone, he'd ended the call and pressed his foot down on the accelerator. If a highway patrolman picked him up for going twenty miles over the speed limit, he'd just have to tell him that an emergency was causing him to speed. And as far as Lonnie was concerned, he wouldn't be lying. If Katherine was upset, it was an emergency to him.

Once he parked in front of the ranch house, his long quick strides ate up the ground from his truck to the front door. When he entered the living room, Katherine was sitting on the couch with David in her arms.

Immediately Lonnie went to stand in front of her. "What's wrong?" he asked without preamble.

The concern on his face and in his voice took her aback for a moment, and all she could do was stare dumbfounded at him.

"What do you mean? Nothing is wrong."

He looped his thumbs over his gun belt and studied her in a way that made Katherine want to squirm. Was this how he questioned the criminals who passed through his jail? If so, they were probably too afraid not to talk.

"Don't lie," he said gruffly. "I could hear it in your voice when I called. Something has upset you."

She let out a long, weary breath. "I thought we were going to town. We don't have time for this."

"Then something *is* wrong. You've practically admitted it."

He sounded so adamant, so disturbed, that she had to release a little laugh. "Lonnie, I'm fine. Yes, I did get a bit…well, shook up. But I'm over it."

Easing down beside her, Lonnie carefully pulled the blanket printed with lambs back from David's cheek. "He looks fine. Has he been crying more than usual?"

Katherine smiled wanly. "He hasn't been crying at all. Not even during his bath. The baby is perfectly all right."

Lonnie's gaze lifted to search Katherine's face. "Are you going to tell me?"

That he could read her so squarely on the button took Katherine by complete surprise. She'd always been a loner, so to speak, and she'd never been one to outwardly display her feelings. The fact that Lonnie knew her well enough to sense that something was wrong told her that the two of them were getting even closer than she'd imagined. And that wasn't a good thing. Not for her.

"All right," she admitted a bit crossly. "I got a phone call."

"Not again! Who wanted to chew on me this time? Dave Parker? He just had a new saddle stolen from his barn and he swears that I know who did it, but that I won't arrest the person. The man—"

"Lonnie," she interrupted with a shake of her head. "It wasn't anyone living here in the county. It was Seth. Seth Ketchum."

His blue eyes opened wide, and Katherine realized she couldn't have shocked him more.

"Seth?" he returned. "Damn it all, the man wasn't supposed to be calling here! Calling you! I told him—"

Seeing he was getting all worked up, Katherine laid a hand on his arm. "Lonnie, it's okay. I don't mind."

That pulled him up short, and he looked at her in total surprise. "You don't?"

She shook her head. "Not really. I can't blame him for wanting to talk to me. He believes—" she stopped and her chin dipped downward as she studied David's sleeping face "—that I'm his sister. He didn't say that exactly. But I knew that's what he was thinking—I could hear it in his voice. Funny how I knew that about him, isn't it?"

"Maybe that's because you truly are his sister," Lonnie said gently.

A pain struck her somewhere in the region of her heart. "I, uh, I don't want to think about that now," she mumbled, then, lifting her face up to his, she gave him a wan smile. "Can we go to town now? I don't want to take up any more of your time than necessary."

He frowned with disbelief. "Damn it, Katherine, would you quit worrying about my time? Why is it that you don't want anyone doing something just for you? Why does that make you uncomfortable?"

Dropping her head again, she fumbled with the baby's blanket. "No one said it did."

Lonnie groaned. "Come on, Katherine, do you think I can't see it all over your face. It bothers you to depend on me for anything. Even helping you with David. Is it because I'm a man?"

"No!" The word rushed out of her too quickly to be persuasive. But Katherine didn't care. What else could she say? How else could she explain to this man that she was afraid to start depending on him? She was afraid to get too close, afraid she would start loving him. "Lonnie, I do appreciate your help. But I don't want you to get the idea that while I'm here, I might take advantage of you, of all you've done for me. I wouldn't want there to be any misunderstanding between us."

Lifting his forefinger to her face, Lonnie traced a gentle little pattern on her cheek. "In other words," he said softly, "you want to keep things friendly but cool between us."

His touch burned like the hot summer sun and, like the sun, it felt good even though she knew it wasn't good for her.

"Lonnie," she whispered desperately. "Don't put me on the spot. I told you—"

"Yeah, you told me," he interrupted. Quickly he rose to his feet and then, bending at the waist, he reached for the baby. "Let me carry him out to the truck for you."

Flustered by the abrupt change in him, Katherine fumbled for a heavy baby blanket lying on the cushion next to her.

"All right. Just a minute," she told him.

After she wrapped the pale-blue blanket around her son, she placed him in Lonnie's strong arms. As he settled the baby comfortably in the crook of his arm, she gathered up her handbag and started for the door. Lonnie followed close on her heels.

By the time her fingers closed around the knob, she couldn't stand the flat, empty feeling inside of her. She turned to him, her expression anguished. "Lonnie, are you angry with me? If you are—I don't want you to be. I—"

"Oh, Katherine!" he gently scolded. "I couldn't be angry with you. Frustrated maybe. But never angry. Don't you understand that? Whether you like it or not, you and I have become more than friends. We're partners."

Partners. That sounded too much like love and marriage to her, yet the soft light in his blue eyes warmed her heart so completely that she couldn't keep from smiling. She couldn't keep from reaching out and sliding her hand into his.

"If you say so, Lonnie."

Chapter Eleven

Because David was still only a few days old, Lonnie thought it would be safer for him to keep the baby in the vehicle while Katherine did her shopping. But Katherine had assured him that with her breast-feeding David, the child's immune system should be strong. Besides, the baby couldn't live in a bubble, she argued.

Lonnie had to finally concede, and the three of them entered the discount store only to be stopped by the greeter at the door, a thin, gray-haired man whom Lonnie had been acquainted with ever since he moved to Hereford.

"Well, Sheriff Corteen, how're y'all today?"

"Dandy, George, just dandy," Lonnie said to the older man. "I like this warmer weather, don't you?"

"Sure do, Sheriff. I can't dance when my bones hurt." He gestured toward the bundle cradled in Lonnie's arms. "Whatcha got there, Sheriff? Looks like a baby to me."

Grinning, Lonnie leaned closer to the man and pulled the blue blanket down far enough to expose David's face. "Just look at him, George. He's named after me. Isn't he a handsome guy?"

The older man's eyes lit up as he looked at the baby, then back and forth between Lonnie and Katherine. "Sure is. My, my. I wish I could peel back a few years so me and Hatti could have us another little one. She's still a mighty sexy dame, but she might have to peel back a few years, too," he joked, then leaning toward Lonnie's ear, he whispered loud enough for even Katherine to hear, "You'd better marry her, Sheriff. She's a pretty one."

Lonnie chuckled. "She might have something to say about that, George."

George cackled as he noticed the red embarrassment on Katherine's face. "Yes, sir. She just might."

Sliding an arm around the back of her waist, Lonnie guided her away from George, toward a row of shopping baskets.

Since he was still holding the baby, Katherine pulled one of the carts loose from the line and plopped her handbag into the front partition. "Do you know everyone in this town?" she asked Lonnie.

"I'm the sheriff. I try to know most everybody."

She smiled. "And they all know that you're single, obviously."

"They'd be pretty blind if they didn't."

Although it was a sunny afternoon, the store wasn't overly crowded with shoppers. Yet as Katherine guided the shopping buggy toward the children's department, she sensed the curious stares of several people along the way. No doubt they were wondering what their county sheriff was doing going around with a woman and a new infant. Especially when he was carrying David and showing him off as if the baby were his own child.

The last thought had her wondering just how it would be if Lonnie really were David's father. Would he always be proud of him? Would he always want to guide and protect him? To teach him all the things a man needed to know when he went out in the world on his own? And what about her, she wondered. Would Lonnie be like the greeter and think she was sexy even when she was old and gray? No. She couldn't imagine any man staying with her for the long haul. The majority of them always left a heartbroken woman behind. Like Walt. And like her father, whoever he was.

"What's the matter? You're scowling. Did George offend you?"

Shaking her thoughts away, Katherine glanced up at him and instantly her heart swelled with an emotion so tender, so full of longing that tears stung her throat. George hadn't offended her. He'd made her dream for things she shouldn't be dreaming of. He'd made her long for things that weren't meant to be hers.

"Of course he didn't offend me. He seemed like a nice old man."

Amusement twinkled in his eyes. "Nice. But a little nosy, huh?"

Her lips twisted. "You're the one who has to live around here. By the time I leave, there's no telling what people will be saying about you."

Lonnie shook his head. "You think that worries me?"

She looked at him drolly. "No."

"You're right. As long as I do my job as a lawman, that's all the folks around here want from me. So let's get to shopping and not worry about the people who might be gossiping about us," he suggested with a little nudge against her back.

Spotting an aisle of infant items, Katherine turned the buggy in that direction. "So it doesn't matter to you if they're saying you've been keeping a single woman with a baby in the house with you?"

Lonnie chuckled. "Who's gonna blame me after they take a look at you?"

His compliment put color in her cheeks and, in an effort to avoid any more remarks on the matter, she quickly put her attention into searching for the baby items she needed.

Thirty minutes later, Katherine had everything on her list and then some. After passing through the checkout, where several of the checkers left their posts to view the baby Sheriff Corteen was holding, the three of them left the building. Once they reached Lonnie's truck, he handed her the baby and began to load the packages in the back compartment of the cab.

He was placing the last bag into the truck when the pager at the side of his hip began to buzz. Mumbling with frustration, he looked at the number, then helped Katherine into the passenger seat.

"Looks like the office is trying to contact me," he told her. "I guess Mitch has come up against something he can't handle."

After Katherine and the baby were settled, Lonnie joined her on the driver's side and quickly reached for the cell phone on the dashboard and punched in a set of numbers.

"Mitch—oh, Scarlett. Where's Mitch? He's supposed to be taking care of things. Who needs me?"

Scarlett quickly answered his question. "Mitch left a few minutes ago, Sheriff. It appears that Eddie Landers is holed up out at his place with a shotgun. Won't let anyone near him."

"Dear God! Is he threatening to harm himself?"

Lonnie's question had Katherine darting a concerned glance at him.

Scarlett went on. "That's what it sounds like, Sheriff. He's out to harm himself or anyone who comes on the place. Mitch and Josh have gone out there in a squad car to try to reason with him, but I think Eddie wants to talk to you."

Lonnie kept his groan to himself. What a time for an old acquaintance to have a mental breakdown.

"All right, Scarlett. I'm already here in town," he told the dispatcher. "I'll head to the office right now. Do you think you could drive Katherine and the baby back out to the ranch for me?"

"Oh, no! Don't put your officer to all that trouble," Katherine said to him in a hushed voice. "We can wait for you."

With his hand over the telephone's mouthpiece, he glanced grimly over at Katherine. "You can't wait. This is an emergency that might take hours. I just don't know yet."

Gauging the serious look on Lonnie's face, Katherine decided the best thing she could do right now was to follow his instructions without argument.

Nodding, she said, "All right."

He quickly relayed the message to Scarlett to be ready to leave the office in a few minutes, then quickly ended the call.

"Can you tell me what's going on?" Katherine asked once he'd put away the cell phone. "You look very worried."

"I am worried, Katherine. An old friend is threatening to shoot himself or anyone who comes near him. I've got to get out there and stop him."

Katherine suddenly froze in her seat. Lonnie might be shot! Or even worse, killed! Just the thought paralyzed her with fear.

"Lonnie! You're the sheriff! You're supposed to be doing administrative work, not facing a maniac with a gun!" she exclaimed.

He looked at her as though she'd suddenly lost her mind. "Hereford isn't some big city, Katherine, where a sheriff sits behind a desk all day, giving orders and signing papers. I'm a working member of the force here, and if that puts me in danger, then that's just a part of the job. Do you think I'd ask my men to do something that I wouldn't do?"

Katherine swallowed hard. She was behaving like a frantic wife. She had to get ahold of herself before he got the idea that she was crazy about him.

"No," she answered meekly.

"Damn right, no."

Her face deathly pale, she reached over and touched his shoulder. "I'm just scared for you, Lonnie. I…don't want to think of anything happening to you."

The concern he heard in her wobbly voice had him

plucking her hand from his shoulder and drawing it to his lips.

Katherine shuddered with longing and fear as he kissed the back of her hand, then turned it over and kissed the palm.

"Don't fret, Katherine. It's going to put wrinkles on your brow."

And if she wasn't careful, *he* was going to put tears in her heart.

She drew in a deep breath and let it out slowly. "Do you know what went wrong with this man? Is it common for him to be violent?"

Lonnie shook his head. "Eddie's one of the kindest, gentlest human beings I know. It would be hard for him to lift his hand to a biting dog."

"Then what do you suppose has happened? Does he have a family?"

Lonnie's glum nod answered her question.

"Yeah. A wife. Two kids. Eddie wouldn't hurt his family. He's been having financial trouble here lately. He lost his corn crop this fall to a bad hail and windstorm. If I were a betting man, I'd say all of this stems from that."

Katherine had to remind herself to keep breathing as her eyes slanted toward the revolver strapped to his hip. "Lonnie, you won't...just try to walk up to him, will you? Even if a person is normally gentle, sometimes they crack under pressure. This man might hurt you."

Reaching across the seat, he lifted her chin with his forefinger. "Don't worry, Katherine. I'm not about to let that happen."

Less than two minutes later Lonnie screeched the truck to a halt outside the sheriff's office.

"Just wait here in the truck," he instructed as he slung off his seat belt. "I'll send Scarlett out to take you home."

As he opened the door and slid to the ground, Katherine couldn't help but call out to him.

Pausing, he glanced questioningly back at her and in that moment Katherine did her best to memorize the rugged lines and planes of his face. She truly cared about this man. If she hadn't known it before, she certainly knew it now. Yet now wasn't the time to reveal her feelings. She wasn't sure there would ever be a time.

"I...I just wanted to say good luck."

"Thanks, Katherine."

With a brief smile, he gave her a little salute before he trotted off toward the front of the building.

Less than five minutes later, a young woman somewhere near Katherine's age, with short, chestnut hair and dressed in a Sheriff's Department uniform hurried toward the truck.

After sliding into the driver's seat, she looked over at Katherine and, with a bright smile, extended her hand.

"Hi. I'm Scarlett O'Grady."

Encouraged by her warm greeting, Katherine firmly shook the other woman's hand. "Nice to meet you. I'm Katherine McBride. And that's my son, Lonnie David, in the child seat in the back."

Instantly Scarlett twisted around in the seat so she could view the baby, and just as instantly she squealed with pleasure at the sight of his cherub face framed with a blue blanket. "Ooooh, he's so cute! He looks like you, I'll bet you've already heard that."

Katherine smiled faintly. "It was one of the first things Lonnie said after little David was born."

Scarlett gave the baby one last look, then turned in the seat and began to fasten the safety belt. "I'd love to take time to hold him. But as you've probably already heard, things are a little crazy around here. I need to get you home and get back here to the station as quickly as possible."

Katherine grimaced as Scarlett put the truck into Reverse and backed onto the street.

"I feel awful about being a nuisance," she told the dispatcher. "I could have driven myself back, but Lonnie seems to think I'm still not up to doing anything the least little bit strenuous."

Scarlett waved a dismissive hand at her. "Oh, don't think anything about it. You're not a nuisance. Emergencies can happen at any hour, day or night. Lonnie's used to them. Everyone on the force is used to them."

The sudden urge to cry had Katherine turning her face toward the passenger window and blinking the moisture away from her eyes. "Do situations like this happen often?"

"You mean like Eddie?" Before Katherine could answer, Scarlett went on, "No. We've had some armed robberies and a shoot-out or two before. But don't worry about Lonnie. He's a good lawman. He's well trained and he knows what to do. That's why the people of Deaf Smith County like him. That, plus the fact that he's just generally nice and fair."

Scarlett's confidence in her boss helped to vanquish the fear that had enveloped Katherine. This professional woman wasn't breaking down at the idea of Lonnie facing a violent man with a shotgun so neither should she. But the awful quaking deep inside her refused to go away.

"How long have you worked for Lonnie?"

"Three years. I've been going to college on the side. I'm trying to earn a law degree, but at the rate I'm going I'll be gray-haired by the time I ever see the inside of a courtroom. That is, as a lawyer," she added with a chuckle.

The young woman negotiated the truck onto a highway that would eventually lead them to the Rafter C. As the town of Hereford disappeared behind them, Katherine thought about her own future.

Before she'd become pregnant with David she'd had all sorts of plans. To go back to college and get a degree in business, maybe even go into the field of money management. She'd dreamed of saving enough money to put down on a little house somewhere near Fort Worth or maybe even move down to the hill country near Fredricksburg or Kerrville. Then Walt had come into her life and she'd begun to picture him in her plans. And it was a nice image, the two of them facing the future together.

Except for Celia, Katherine had never had anyone to love her and spend time with her. Just having Walt as a constant companion had made her happy, and she'd faced each day with an eagerness she'd never felt before. Back then, becoming Walt's lover had seemed like the natural progression of things. He'd assured her over and over that he'd found his one true love in her and that as soon as he saved enough money, the two of them would get married.

Katherine had sincerely believed him, and she'd planned and looked forward to the day when she would have a family of her own. They would have a real father who adored them. Her children wouldn't have to wonder who their father was or why he'd not cared enough to be a part of their lives.

The corners of her lips turned down with mocking regret. Those plans seemed so foolish now, and in spite of having little David, she felt more alone than she'd ever felt in her life.

"Do you have a family around here?" Katherine forced herself to ask, more to make conversation than anything.

"Not a husband or children yet. But I belong to a big family. And they're always trying to tell me what to do and how to do it. Sometimes they can really get on my nerves. Especially my brothers and sister. But Lonnie is always quick to remind me how lucky I am. And when I stop and look at him, I realize that I am lucky." She cast a pointed glance in Katherine's direction. "You know, he doesn't have anybody. That's why all of us on the force were thrilled when we heard about you."

Katherine's brows inched upward. "Me? I'm just here for a few days."

"Oh. Is that all? We all thought—well, with Lonnie carrying on so about the baby and you naming him Lonnie David—we thought there had to be something between the two of you. Is there?"

Katherine wasn't used to people she'd only just met being so blunt with their questions. Yet Scarlett's curiosity didn't offend her, it only made her cogitate even harder. Was there something between herself and Lonnie? He'd said so. He'd said the two of them were partners. But what kind of partners and how soon was their partnership going to come to an end?

"I, uh, I really like Lonnie. A lot. But I don't believe either one of us is ready for something—serious."

"Hmm. I don't get it. What's stopping you? Unless—" She paused and glanced thoughtfully at Katherine. "Oh, I wasn't thinking. I guess you must still be involved with the baby's father."

Katherine stiffened at the very thought. "No! Not at all!"

Scarlett shot her a surprised look. "Then I guess I really don't get it. If you like Lonnie 'a lot' then what's stopping you from getting serious? Or don't you think he's a hunk? I sure do. But we're just friends, you know, like brother and sister."

Glancing down at her lap, Katherine realized her hands were clamped together in a tight knot. She purposely separated them and tried to clear the huskiness from her throat. "Believe me, Scarlett, I noticed right off what a wonderful guy Lonnie is, but I've been through a lot these past few months. I don't want to make any more mistakes."

Scarlett's brows inched upward. "And you think you'd be making a mistake if you got involved with Lonnie?"

Yes! No! Dear God, she didn't know anymore. At this moment she was more frightened for his safety than anything. "I don't know, Scarlett. I just don't know."

Once they arrived at the Rafter C, Scarlett helped Katherine get the baby and all the packages into the house before she jumped back into the truck and took off at full speed in the direction of town.

Feeling as though she'd been lifted up by a tornado, then suddenly dropped back to earth, Katherine tried to collect her senses as she put David to bed in his bassinet and stowed away the things she'd purchased in town. Yet she couldn't settle her nerves, and it was only a matter of minutes before she was up and walking the floor.

For once, the quietness of the house only added to the tension that twisted every muscle in her body. Out of desperation she clicked on the television and hoped one of the local news services had picked up on the standoff. But of course the closest channel was broadcast from Amarillo and it wouldn't have had time to send a news crew this far away. So she waited and watched and imagined Lonnie in all sorts of terrifying situations. And imagined, too, how she would feel if he were taken from this earth.

His job as a sheriff had never struck her as being overly dangerous until today, until she'd seen with her own eyes that he was more than a figurehead, he was a hands-on lawman. How did a woman deal with this kind of fear, the fear of losing her man?

Stop it, Katherine! Lonnie isn't your man. He isn't yours to lose.

The little voice yelling at her stiffened her spine, yet it did little to relieve her shaky hands and stop her urge to pace through the small house. Eventually, David must have picked up on her disturbed state of mind. He woke long before his normal nap time was over and began to fuss loudly.

Katherine changed his diaper and let him nurse, but even that didn't seem to satisfy her son. After several attempts to rock him back to sleep, he finally gave in to the gentle movement and the soft lullaby she sang to him. But he didn't stay asleep for long, and she spent the remainder of the afternoon carrying and patting and rocking the fussy baby.

By the time darkness had fallen, she was exhausted. Not just from dealing with David's crankiness, but from the constant worry and wonder about Lonnie's safety. So far she hadn't heard anything on the television or the radio, and Katherine was on the verge of making a nuisance of herself and calling the Sheriff's Department when she heard a vehicle pull to a stop outside the house.

Rushing to the living room, she swung open the front door just as Lonnie was about to open it. The unexpected movement caught him off guard and caused him to stumble forward over the threshold.

"Whoa, girl!" He caught her by the shoulders just as he steadied himself on his feet. "I nearly fell right on you. Are you all right?"

She took one look at his dear face and burst into sobs. "Oh, Lonnie! Lonnie!"

With one hand, he reached behind him and shut the door. With the other hand, he drew her against his chest.

"Aw, honey, now what's the matter?" he asked softly. "I've never seen such a fountain of tears."

Flinging her arms around his waist, she held on to him tightly and thought she'd never felt anything as good as his rock-hard body, she'd never smelled anything as heady as the unique scent of his hair and skin.

"I've been so worried about you. I kept waiting to hear what happened and when I didn't I was afraid something horrible had happened to you!"

She was clinging to him as if she would never let him go, and as Lonnie looked down at her head buried against the middle of his chest, he felt his heart burgeoning with an emotion that couldn't be mistaken or ignored.

He loved this woman. Loved her with every particle of his being. No matter what happened between them in the future, those feelings would never change.

"Katherine. My little darling, you shouldn't have worried. I'm fine. It's all over. Eddie's been taken to a place where he can be treated." He brought his fingertips beneath her chin and tilted her face up to his. "See? I'm too ornery to get hurt."

She tried to sniff away her tears. But in spite of the effort, the salty stream continued to flow down her cheeks. "There's not a ornery bone in your body, Lonnie Corteen," she said in a weepy, accusing voice.

Chuckling under his breath, he gathered her close against him and simply held her for a long moment. "Some people might give you a debate over that, Katherine." He brought a hand up and stroked the back of her head. As he pushed his fingers through the silken strands of her hair, he asked in a voice that was full of both amusement and reproach, "Were you really that worried about me?"

Instantly she tilted her face up so that she could look at him. The disbelief she saw in his expression both amazed and angered her. He didn't have a clue as to how much she'd suffered during these agonizing hours!

"You big lug!" she exclaimed as she gripped the front of his shirt. "I've been worried out of my mind. You could have been shot, maimed, killed! I've been going around here for hours nearly pulling my hair out!"

"Oh, honey, I didn't want you to worry. But—" He stopped and grinned at her, a grin that was decidedly wicked. "I'm sure glad to know you care that much about me."

As soon as his words were out, Katherine's lips parted with sudden dawning. Darn it, what had she been thinking? She might as well have been telling the man she'd fallen in love with him. And she hadn't! She wasn't about to expose herself or her little boy to that much pain.

"I didn't say…I do care, but not in the way you're thinking," she said as she attempted to twist out of his arms.

Lonnie tightened his hold on her back and at the same time bent his head toward hers. "Really?" he countered softly. "I think you do care. And I think right now you're wanting to kiss me, just as much as I want to kiss you."

How could she deny his suggestion when all day she'd longed, prayed for the chance to see him, touch him again.

"I—oh, yes, Lonnie." She breathed the concession as she tilted her face up to his.

With a gravelly growl, he brought his lips down over hers, and for a moment Katherine was stunned motionless as the incredible taste of him swept through her senses like a strong, wild wind. She wanted this man!

She'd wanted him since the first time he'd walked into her apartment.

When he felt her arms sliding up around her neck, when he felt her mouth opening, inviting him for more, Lonnie eased his head back and looked into her green eyes. "I'm sorry I couldn't let you know sooner that I was okay and all had ended well. But then maybe I wouldn't have gotten this sort of greeting from you. And right now, this is all that matters."

This was a kiss that utterly consumed her body and her mind. As his lips rocked back and forth over hers, heat began to soar through her body, collect in her breasts, her belly and loins.

The urge to have her body next to his had her squirming closer, sliding her hands to the middle of his chest and working the buttons loose on his shirt.

When she slipped her hands inside and flattened them against his heated skin, he eased his lips away from hers and sucked in a sharp breath.

"We, uh, we need to get out of the doorway," he whispered.

Before the interruption of the kiss could cool her back to sanity, he bent and picked her up in his arms. She clung to his shoulders until he levered her down in an armchair angled to one side of the fireplace. Then, resting on his knees in front of her, he clasped her face between his palms and lowered his mouth back to hers.

Moaning deep in her throat, Katherine arched upward in the chair, circled her arms around his waist and tugged him toward her. The weight of his body smashed her backward against the cushion, but she didn't mind the faint crimp in her neck or the fact that she was imprisoned between him and the chair. As long as he was touching her, kissing her that was all she cared about.

"Katherine," he murmured against her throat. "Sweet Katherine. I want to make love to you. I've wanted that from the very first time I met you."

She pushed against his shoulders. "But I was pregnant then!" she exclaimed.

He grinned ruefully. "I can't help that. You were beautiful and sexy. Just as you are now."

To prove his point, he lifted the hem of her sweater and exposed her plump little belly.

Katherine sucked in a sharp breath as he lowered his head and pressed several kisses around her navel, then worked his way up the middle of her midriff. Sliding his fingers across her back, he fumbled with the catch on her bra until the two pieces of fabric fell apart and he could push the garment up and over her breasts.

As soon as they were exposed to his sight, Lonnie cupped the precious weight of them in his hands. They were lush and full, the nipples moist and engorged. He tasted their sweetness until he felt her fingers raking against his scalp, holding him to her with a fierceness that echoed the throbbing ache of his manhood.

His fingers found the zipper at the front of her pants, and he tugged it downward until he could slip his whole hand inside. As his palm cupped the mound of her femininity, his lips traveled back to hers, where he suckled and bit and coaxed her tongue to slip inside his mouth.

Slowly his fingers traveled downward until they reached the juncture of her thighs and the moist folds of her womanhood. As he gently probed and teased,

Katherine felt the heat of wanting him building, magnifying until she thought she would explode.

Tearing her lips from his, she whimpered, "Lonnie…we…I can't…"

"Shh," he whispered urgently against her throat, "I know you can't make love yet. Just let me pleasure you. Let me do that much for you."

Katherine couldn't argue with him. She wanted him, needed him too much to move from his embrace.

"Lonnie, Lonnie," she murmured against his lips. "I want you so!"

"I know, honey. I'm feeling just what you're feeling."

Moaning, she opened her lips over his. Immediately he took the initiative, plundering her lips with his and exploring the warm, moist cavern of her mouth with his tongue. At the same time, his fingers slipped inside her and began to move in a slow, seductive rhythm.

Katherine tried not to respond, tried to hold on to the tiny scrap of sanity left in her senses, but she was hungry with desire and he was feeding her with a sweetness, a gentleness she'd never experienced before. In only a matter of moments she felt a spring inside her growing tighter and tighter until finally the incredible tension snapped and she split into a million golden pieces.

"Oh! Ohh! Lonnie!" Jerking straight up in the chair, she buried her face in his shoulder and shuddered with an ecstasy that was almost too much to bear.

Chapter Twelve

Several moments passed before Katherine's senses began working again, and when they did she realized Lonnie was murmuring her name over and over and his hands were gliding through her hair, stroking her back.

Dear heaven, what had she done? She'd let him make love to her in such an intimate way!

The shock of her wanton response filled her face with fiery embarrassment. With a self-deprecating groan she pushed against his shoulders and scrambled from the armchair.

By the time Lonnie caught up with her, she was in the bedroom sitting on the side of the bed, her head bent, her face covered with both hands.

"Katherine?"

When she didn't respond, he walked quietly into the room and took a seat beside her.

Laying a hand on her knee, he asked, "Katherine? Do you hate me that much?"

His question was so absurd it startled her, and she looked up at him with wide, teary eyes.

"I could never hate you. Never," she whispered emphatically.

Clearly bewildered by her behavior, his blue eyes scanned her troubled face. "Then why did you run from me like that? Are you ashamed of what we just did? Do you regret letting me touch you?"

No! Yes! Oh, how could she explain, she wondered frantically. How could she tell him that what she'd just experienced with him was so incredible it frightened her.

"No," she answered bluntly. "I don't regret it. I—" She paused and blinked as moisture began to build in her eyes. "I'm just a little overwhelmed, that's all. You see, I've never felt that way with any man before. Not even David's father. And I guess——" Taking a deep, ragged breath, she glanced away from him. "I guess it scares me, Lonnie. It scares me a whole lot."

Leaning closer, he pushed the dark, tangled hair away from her cheeks, then pressed his lips against her temple. "There's nothing to be afraid of, Katherine. I'm not going to hurt you. I could never hurt you."

She sucked in another shaky breath and tried to ignore the urge to bury her face against his chest. If she was ever going to be strong, she had to be iron willed now. Otherwise, her heart would have her agreeing to anything this man proposed.

"I've been told that before," she said softly.

Silent seconds ticked by and then he said in a lightly accusing voice, "You think I'm just spouting words."

Her face jerked around to his and she looked at him with a pained expression. "No! I'm—no, I don't think you'd lie to me. And I don't think you'd ever deliberately set out to hurt me, but…things happen. People change."

A groan of frustration slipped past his lips. "Look, Katherine, I'll admit that a few minutes ago, I got carried away and so did you. What happened between us wasn't something I'd planned!"

"I didn't say it was," she countered swiftly. Shoving her hair back from her forehead, she jumped to her feet and began to pace back and forth in front of him. "Lonnie, I'm sorry. I can see that I'm not explaining myself very well. But I don't know how to explain what I'm feeling—except that I'm very afraid. Not of you. But of myself. And of taking steps that I'm just not ready to take. Do you understand?"

Reaching out, he snagged one of her hands and pulled her toward him. She stumbled awkwardly forward until she was standing between his parted legs and his hands were tightly clenched at the sides of her waist.

"Of course I understand," he said roughly. "Do you think I've forgotten what it's like to be deceived and fooled into thinking you're loved and then to be abandoned like some unwanted dog with the mange? I didn't just have that happen to me with Ginger. I had it happen when I was only seven years old! My own mother left me! And to this day she's never come back. You think living through something like that makes a man brave? Do you think I *want* to hold my heart out and say, Here it is, see if you can break it again?"

Hanging her head, she swallowed against the pain squeezing around her heart. This was wrong, she thought miserably, all wrong. Two scarred people couldn't merge to make one strong, sensible link.

To him she mumbled, "I know that you've been hurt, Lonnie. And I hate that. I wish none of it had ever happened to you. But—" she lifted her head and met his solemn gaze "—I'm not so sure you're any more ready for a relationship than I am."

He said flatly, "You don't know what I'm ready for."

Feeling cornered and desperate, she said in a rush, "I need to get back to Fort Worth. I've stayed here too long."

Stunned, he stared at her. "Too long?" he repeated with disbelief. "You've only been here a week!"

She started to pull away, but he wouldn't allow it, so she stood there between his legs and tried not to look at his strong, broad shoulders, the tanned rugged features of his face, the dark-blue depths of his eyes.

"I realize it's only been a week. But can't you see what's happening between us? We're—well, neither of us is thinking straight. And, if I stay here longer—"

"I'm thinking very straight," he interrupted. "Today a friend wanted to shoot himself and anyone who got in his path. And you know why?"

Katherine shook her head. "You said he was in financial trouble."

"That started the problem. But Eddie's real concern was his wife and children. He was so afraid of losing them that he snapped."

"How did you find this out? He talked to you?"

Lonnie nodded soberly. "And you know, Katherine, as he talked, I kept thinking, I can relate to this guy. I understood what he was thinking and feeling and why he was so desperate. I realized how devastated I would be if you left."

The words stunned her, and for long moments she couldn't speak. Finally she shook her head and stuttered, "Lonnie…don't. I'm not sure I want to hear this."

His hands tugged her closer until her belly was pressed against his chest and his head was bent backward so that he could see her face. "I love you, Katherine. I love you and David both. Maybe that doesn't mean much to you. But I'm hoping it does. I'm hoping you'll stay here and let the three of us be a family."

He loved her! This wonderful man loved her!

A part of Katherine wanted to shout with a joy she'd never felt before, but the sensible part of her was already beginning to shed a pool of silent tears. Maybe Lonnie did love her right at this moment, she rationalized. Maybe he'd love her for the next two weeks or even two years. But eventually his feelings would wither away. In due course, he'd realize she wasn't the woman he'd believed her to be and then he'd be gone, just like Walt. There had to be some sort of flaw in her, she thought, something that made the men in her life decide she wasn't worth the effort. Heck, even Noah Rider hadn't cared enough to admit that he was her father, much less stick around to *be* one to her. What could possibly make her believe Lonnie would be any different?

Bringing her hands to his face, she cupped his strong jaw in her palms. "I'm not convinced it's love you feel for me, Lonnie. But whatever it is, I'm very flattered that you care. And I'm very beholden to you for all you've done: delivering the baby, taking care of us both, opening your home to us. I'll never forget any of it—or you."

His hands loosened their grip and began to slide gently up and down her rib cage. I hear a *but* in there, Katherine. Why?"

A ragged sigh slipped from her throat. Then, closing her eyes, she pulled away from his grasp and crossed the room. As she stared unseeingly out the darkened window, she said, "I'm just not ready for any of this, Lonnie. I'm not sure that I ever will be."

The mattress creaked as he rose from his seat. As he walked up behind her, Katherine braced herself for his touch. But the feel of his strong hands never came. Instead, his low, steady voice brushed close to her ear.

"Why, Katherine? Because you're terrified that I'll dump you? Are you going to turn down something good because you can't see past your fear?"

Swallowing, she wondered how long she would miss this man, how long would she carry this empty hole around in her heart? "I don't want to be this way, Lonnie."

"And I don't want you to go. Tell me you're not going—at least not for the next few days."

Her throat was aching with tears. Deep, raw emotions gripped her until she thought she was going to die from it.

"I can't make promises," she whispered huskily.

He cleared his throat and then fell silent for long moments. Katherine's heart pounded with dread and pain as she waited for him to berate her, to tell her she was heartless.

But those words never came, instead he said, "Katherine, you're forgetting you came out here to think about the Ketchums, to find out more about them. You haven't done that yet. We haven't even discussed them or the possibility of you being Amelia's daughter."

The Ketchums. She couldn't belong to that family any more than she could belong to Lonnie. It wasn't meant for her to belong to anyone!

"I—other things happened. The Ketchums aren't important now. I have a son to care for and—" She stopped in midsentence as David's cry sounded from the living room. "Excuse me, I'd better go see about him."

Katherine slept poorly that night and not just because David was fussing with colic. Even when the baby slept, she was rolling and tumbling in the bed, her mind consumed with Lonnie and the sad conclusion that she had to leave the ranch. By the time morning arrived, she woke groggy and drained.

After several cups of coffee, she stepped into the shower with the firm decision that she couldn't stay here on the Rafter C any longer. Her reckless behavior last night proved that she couldn't risk spending another day, even another hour, in Lonnie's presence.

By midmorning, she'd called the bus station for the schedule that would take her all the way back to Fort Worth. After that she'd managed to pack all of her and David's things and load them into Lonnie's old ranch truck, a '68 Ford that had once been black but was now faded to a chalky gray. It was a standard shift and she wasn't certain that she could find the gears, but she was going to do her damnedest to drive the thing. There was no way she was going to call Lonnie and ask him to drive her to the bus station. Not only would he argue against her leaving, she just couldn't bear saying good-bye face-to-face. It would tear her heart out.

Katherine had been so focused on packing during the morning that she didn't find the note Lonnie had left on the coffee table until she was almost ready to leave the house. Actually, it was more than a note; it was a large manila envelope with her name scrawled across the front.

Picking it up, she eased down on the couch next to David's bassinet. The baby had been awake for the last fifteen or twenty minutes and so far, in spite of jostling him around, he'd been quiet and content. Hopefully his bout with colic was over and he wouldn't set up a big howl on the bus. Not everyone could deal with a crying baby.

Oh well, if worse came to worst, she'd get off the bus at the nearest town available and call Althea to come get her. The woman was the one friend Katherine could call on in good times or bad.

"We're going to be on our way pretty soon, my little darling." She planted a soft kiss on David's forehead, then gazed sadly around the room. "This is where you were born," she said to the baby. "And you're probably thinking this is home. And I'm sure you're thinking that big guy that takes you in his arms and rocks you to sleep is your daddy. But he isn't, honey. We've got to make our own home back in Fort Worth."

The baby was enthralled by his mother's voice. Still and quiet, his eyes tried to focus on her face. But as soon as her last words died away, he puckered his bow-shaped lips and wailed loudly.

With a loving groan, Katherine lifted him from the basket and cradled him in her arms. Swaying him gently, she sang him a little tune about rainbows and blue skies and how every day of his life was going to be a sunny day. He soon fell asleep, and she placed him gently back into the rattan basket.

Once she'd finished carefully covering him with a blanket, she turned her attention to the envelope on her lap. Opening it, she turned it upside down on the cushion next to her. Two smaller envelopes fell out, a folded newspaper clipping, along with a glossy snapshot, and one sheet of lined paper creased in the middle.

Reaching for the paper first, she opened it and read:

Dearest Katherine,
You said the Ketchums aren't important to you now. But that's because you haven't met them yet. You don't know what a wonderful family you're turning your back on. They want you to be a part of their lives. Maybe when you're able to understand that, you'll also understand how much I love you.
Lonnie

Tears rolled from her eyes and she had to wipe them away before she could examine the two envelopes. With shaky hands, she turned each one of them over until the address was facing her. Both of them had been mailed to Amelia Tucker from Celia. Katherine recognized the old return address as being the one where they used to live here in Hereford when she'd been a small child.

Taking a deep, bracing breath, she pulled the small, handwritten pages from the envelope with the oldest postage date. As she began to read, the words were warm and loving and written as though Celia was speaking to someone she was very close to. Snippets of local news were relayed and brief details of the recent weather.

Katherine quickly scanned through the small talk until she reached a paragraph that stunned her.

Gripping the paper, her heart began to thud with heavy anticipation as she read on:

Noah came by yesterday to see his daughter. He said that Tucker had sent him to pick up a horse down at Clovis, but he went far off his route and missed a lot of sleep to drive over here to Hereford. There's no doubt that he adores Katherine. I can see it on his face every time he holds her in his arms. And the way he talks about you— well, it just breaks my heart that the two of you can't be together. Especially when I know how much you love him.

I can't understand your reasoning for staying with Tucker. He's a hard-nosed bastard in my book, but I guess when you have four children with someone, there's a tie there that can't be broken. I promise he'll never hear anything from me about you and Noah, or the baby you had together. As far as he knows, you came down here to Hereford to help nurse me through chemotherapy treatments. He'll never know that you had a baby while you were here or that you gave the little one to me to rear as my own. That'll be our secret, sis, always.

It's clear that you can't bring yourself to give

up your other four children to go and live with Noah and Katherine. But as far as I'm concerned, a woman shouldn't have to make such a hard choice. When I think about you, sis, it isn't hard for me to swear off men. I don't want any of the heartache or pain you've been going through.

Katherine read a little more, but the letter turned to other, more mundane things, so she laid it aside and picked up the next envelope. This one was postmarked a few years later. By now Katherine was in elementary school. Noah had quit his job as foreman for the T Bar K, yet from Celia's words, he was still keeping up with Katherine's life. As for Amelia, her health was becoming a problem and she was finding it harder and harder to make the trips down to Hereford to see her daughter.

Trips to see her daughter? Katherine thought back to when she was eight, ten and twelve. There had been a woman who'd come to visit from time to time, she remembered. Celia had called her what, Laura? No, Lia. She'd been a quiet, dark-headed woman with a sad air about her. Katherine had always looked forward to her visits because she often took Celia and her shopping for shoes and clothing. And when the two women had cooked meals in the kitchen, Lia always invited Katherine to help with whatever she was doing.

Allowing the yellowed pages to drop to her lap, Katherine closed her eyes against the myriad of emotions parading through her. Strangely, she felt loved and yet abandoned at the same time. She felt deceived and cheated and very, very sad. There was no way she

could doubt that she was Amelia Ketchum and Noah
Rider's child. She was the product of an illicit affair, and
the woman who'd mothered Katherine for all those
years had not really been her mother at all.

Her hands shaking, Katherine shoved the letters back
into the envelopes and started to push the snapshot in
after them, but curiosity caused her to pause just long
enough to glimpse a group gathered somewhere out-of-
doors beneath the shade of a cottonwood tree.

Slowly she righted the photo in her hands and stared
at the people behind the smiling faces. They all appeared older than she was now, somewhere in their thir-
ties. There were two men and one woman, all with hair
a different shade of brunette, and all impressively handsome. Although the woman was slender, she was obviously pregnant. The camera had snapped the man to the
left of her in the act of rubbing her barely protruding
belly. The whole scene was happy and loving, and
Katherine felt a pang of loss just looking at it.

Flipping the photo over, she saw that someone had
printed names and a date on the back. Ross, Victoria and
Seth. September 2003.

Her half brothers. Her half sister. Oh, what would it
be like to be a part of their lives and their love?

Shaking her head, she pushed the photo back into the
manila envelope and out of her sight. She didn't want
to know the answers to those questions. Not ever having something was far better than having it and then losing it. Maybe Lonnie would understand that, once she
was gone and he'd had plenty of time to think about
things.

Leaning forward, she placed the manila envelope

back onto the coffee table and started to rise to her feet. As she did, she spotted the folded newspaper clipping lying on the couch next to her thigh. For a brief moment she considered slipping the paper back into the envelope without ever looking at it. But curiosity got the better of her and she settled back onto the couch and opened the piece of newsprint.

Most of the page had been left intact. At the top she could see it was the front page from the *Aztec Gazette* in New Mexico. The headline was printed in big black type:

DAWSON ARRESTED FOR T BAR K MURDER.

Gripping the paper, Katherine scooted to the edge of the seat and quickly began to read:

Late yesterday evening, San Juan county resident and longtime rancher Rube Dawson was arrested for the murder of Noah Rider. For the past four months the San Juan County Sheriff's department has been working to uncover who had killed the one-time foreman of the T Bar K ranch.

The body of Noah Rider, sixty-seven and a Hereford, Texas, resident, was discovered on T Bar K property back in late spring. Later, it was discovered Rider had been shot in the head by a small-caliber weapon. Although Sheriff Perez hasn't released any statements yet as to the motive of the crime, the *Gazette* has learned from a trusted source that Dawson shot and killed Rider over blackmail payments.

The words began to rush up at Katherine as she continued to read how Dawson had somehow known about Noah and Amelia's affair and about the child that had resulted from it. For years Dawson had demanded payments from Noah to keep the secret from reaching the Ketchums. But once Tucker and Amelia were both dead, Noah decided he wasn't going to allow Dawson to extort another penny from him. He'd met with Dawson to tell him the payments were ending. Instead, his life had ended at the hands of his blackmailer.

Oh God, Katherine silently cried. Noah—her father had been killed because he'd loved a married woman, because he'd had a child with her. And Katherine was that child!

Tears sprang to her eyes, and for long minutes she couldn't stop the hot flow from streaking down her face. Nor could she stem the quaking that had started deep inside her and worked outward to her hands.

Why had Lonnie left this information for her to find? Did he think the tragic evidence would make her change her mind and stay here on the ranch with him, she wondered incredulously. As far as she was concerned, it only proved that love rarely worked. It not only caused people pain, it caused them to be killed!

With grim determination, Katherine went to find a pen and paper to write Lonnie a goodbye note.

Three weeks later, Lonnie stared pensively out the window of his office at the sight of the town's Christmas lights and decorated trees. He'd always loved the holidays and, as sheriff, each year he enjoyed helping his deputies hand out toys to the needy children of the area.

So far this year the department had received a fat amount of donations for the cause, and yesterday he'd sent Scarlett and Mitch on a toy-buying mission. Scarlett had invited Lonnie to join them, but he'd quickly declined, using the excuse that he had too much paperwork to catch up on, which had been partly true. He was always behind on his paperwork. Yet the real truth of the matter was that he didn't want to walk through the children's aisles and be reminded of little David. He missed the baby something awful, and having Katherine gone had left a giant hole in him that just wouldn't heal.

With a heavy sigh he wearily rubbed a hand over his face. Somewhere deep in his heart he'd always known that Katherine would leave him. After all, anybody he'd ever cared for had bade him a final *adios*. Katherine was no different. Yet the day he'd gone home and found her things gone and her note, lying next to the Ketchum letters on the coffee table, he'd felt as though two hands were shoving against his chest, pushing the very air from his lungs.

These past weeks since she'd been gone, a part of him had hoped, prayed that once she got used to the idea of belonging to a family, she would see that the three of them belonged together. But so far that hadn't happened, and he wondered wretchedly if the tax assessor was already working to change Katherine's mind about the two of them having a relationship.

Damn it, maybe she would be better off with the guy, Lonnie thought, as he folded his arms across his chest and leaned a shoulder into the window facing. The man probably had plenty of money to buy her things, to give her a nice house and car. Most likely, he even had enough to put away for David's college. Nope, there wouldn't be any scraping for their children's futures. The guy was almost certainly set up for a family. And being in politics, he more than likely belonged to an elite social circle. As his wife, Katherine would be invited to the nicer events of Fort Worth. And the tax man sure couldn't go wrong showing off a wife like Katherine. She was already a knockout. Duded up in fancy clothes, she would be breathtaking. But would all of that make Katherine happy? Was that the kind of life she wanted?

God, he prayed not. From what he could see, she was not a material person. In fact, she was driven by her emotions almost too much. Otherwise she would already have let go of all those fears she was carrying around inside of her.

"Sheriff? You got a minute?"

The sound of Mitch's voice turned Lonnie's head just in time to see the young deputy entering his office.

"Sure, Mitch. You need something?"

Mitch waved a single paper in his hand. "Just a John Hancock on this request for a search warrant. The one about the stolen four-wheelers."

Moving away from the window, Lonnie motioned for the deputy to join him at the wide desk. As Lonnie sat down and reached for a pen, Mitch leaned his hip on the corner of the desktop.

"Me and Scarlett had a good time buying all those toys yesterday," he said. "You should have gone with us. Maybe it would have put a smile on your face."

Lonnie didn't look up as he scratched his name and the

date at the bottom of the page, but once he was finished, he shoved the paper toward Mitch and looked up at him.

"You think I need to be smiling?" Lonnie asked.

A sheepish expression crossed Mitch's face and he shrugged one shoulder. "It would be a damn sight better than that glower you've been going around with."

Lonnie hadn't realized he'd been glowering. Had anyone else in the department noticed his mood besides Mitch?

"Sorry. I'll practice in the mirror tonight. Maybe I'll look better to you tomorrow."

Picking up the paper from Lonnie's desk, Mitch muttered an oath under his breath. "I don't get it, Sheriff. If you were that crazy about the woman, why did you let her leave?"

Mitch had never been bashful about speaking his mind, even to his superiors. So it hardly surprised Lonnie now. What did surprise Lonnie was the fact that the young man didn't have to ask what his problem was. He'd already concluded it was Katherine.

He arched one brow at the deputy. "I didn't *let* her go, Mitch. If you remember, you and Lester found my old Ford parked down at the bus station. Damn it, I should have hidden the keys," he muttered more to himself than to Mitch.

"Well," Mitch said in an attempt to make his boss feel better. "I guess if the woman wanted to leave that bad, she would have found some way to do it, whether she had the truck keys or not."

A wincing pain hit Lonnie's heart. He couldn't believe Katherine had wanted to get away from him that badly. Especially after the way she'd kissed him and touched him as though she loved him.

Hell, Ginger had done a lot of touching, too. But she hadn't felt one iota of love for him. Maybe Katherine was the same. Maybe he'd been duped again.

"Yeah, you're probably right," Lonnie said. Releasing a heavy breath, he rose from the desk and plucked his hat from its resting place on the wall. "If nothing else is going on, I think I'll head home. I've got a lot of feeding to do."

Mitch didn't make a move to leave the corner of the desk. Instead, he eyed Lonnie with quiet concern. "You know, Sheriff, I really like women."

The offhand remark caused Lonnie to bark out a mocking laugh. "That's hardly a news alert."

Mitch absently tapped the warrant request against his thigh as he watched Lonnie lever his Stetson down on his head.

"No. Don't guess it is," Mitch agreed. "What I'm trying to say is that I like being with them. Really like it. But I've never been in love with one. If it feels anything like I think it might, I don't believe I'd want to lose her. I think I'd fight to get her back. Come hell or high water."

Lonnie grimaced. "And how would you do that, Romeo? The woman made it pretty clear how she felt about me by going back to Fort Worth. I'd be a fool to believe she might come back here to Hereford just for me."

"Maybe not. But you talked her into coming here before."

Reaching for his coat, Lonnie shrugged the fleece-lined garment over his shoulders. "Yeah. But I had a persuasive reason then. The Ketchums. But she's not interested in them. Not any more than she's interested in me."

With long, determined strides, Lonnie left the office and the worried deputy staring after him. Once he reached the ranch house, he went straight to the barn and fed the livestock, then loaded a truck bed full of hay and hauled it out to a herd of cattle that were pastured a long distance from the ranch house.

By the time he returned, it was well after dark and the temperature was nosediving. A hot shower helped to warm him and then he went to the kitchen and made himself a small supper.

A sandwich of cold cuts and a pile of tortilla chips sure couldn't compare to eating Katherine's cooking. But then nothing about the ranch was the same since she and the baby had left. He'd asked himself over and over if the place had always been this quiet and lonely. Had he just not noticed before? Or had Katherine and baby David made him see this home of his in a different light?

Hell, what a question, Corteen, he mentally cursed as he carried the boring meal to the living room. Of course they'd made him see things in a different light! They'd changed his whole world by bringing the place alive with sights and scents and sounds that had filled him with joy. At the end of the day, coming home to the two of them was all he'd thought about. And now with them gone, it was still all he thought about.

With a glum sigh, he switched on the television set and settled back to eat his sandwich. But after a couple of minutes, his concentration left the food and the television screen and his gaze settled on the armchair where he and Katherine had made love.

Maybe it hadn't been love in the technical sense, but

it had been love to Lonnie. And he sure as hell didn't want to think of any other man sharing such an intimate experience with her. Not even that damn tax man.

Placing his uneaten meal on the coffee table, he bent his head and scrubbed his face with both hands.

What was he going to do? What could he do to change Katherine's mind? If he'd been a ladies' man like Mitch he might have several ideas of what to say to make her see they belonged together. But he wasn't a charmer or a ladies' man. He was just a nice guy. And he knew better than anyone that nice guys always finished last.

You've always been a real nice guy, Lonnie. But sometimes you have to take a different approach with women.

Funny how Ethan Hamilton's advice had stuck with him all these years. Lonnie had been Ethan's young deputy when the Lincoln County sheriff had been going through a love affair with the local judge of the same county. His friend had gone through hell trying to convince the woman to marry him. But eventually she'd come around to Ethan's way of thinking and in due time she'd born him a set of twins right at Christmas.

Perhaps he should call Ethan and ask his advice. Maybe the other man could tell him he should go to Fort Worth, throw Katherine over his shoulder and bring her back home. Or he might simply tell Lonnie to forget her. If she'd already left him once, she wasn't worth the effort of going after her a second time.

Lonnie reached for the phone, then just as quickly let his arm drop back to his side. Ethan was a smart guy, but he couldn't tell Lonnie what to do. No more than

Mitch could. Only Lonnie's heart could do that, and right now it was telling him he needed to give Katherine a little Christmas surprise.

Chapter Thirteen

The next afternoon in Fort Worth, Katherine agreed to meet Althea at the courthouse. Her friend had arranged to have her lunch hour expanded to two hours so the two women could grab a quick meal and do a bit of shopping at a nearby mall. Julie was going to be in a Christmas play at school, and Althea needed to find something at the craft store to make a pair of silver wings for an angel costume. Katherine was hardly a seamstress, but since she'd returned to Fort Worth, she'd not had the chance to visit with Althea for more than fifteen minutes at a time and most of those chats had taken place over the phone. She needed to get out of the apartment. And an hour spent with her friend might help lift her spirits. God only knew how low they'd been since she'd left the Rafter C.

For the outing she dressed David in a pair of tiny

denim overalls and a red-and-blue-striped T-shirt. As for herself, she really didn't care what she looked like. However, she didn't want to embarrass Althea by wearing a pair of old jeans and a grungy sweatshirt, so she dressed in a pair of winter-white slacks and a matching sweater. And in an effort to be festive for the coming holiday, she pinned a striped candy cane to her shoulder and pulled her dark hair back with a red scarf.

After wasting several minutes in an effort to find a parking spot near the courthouse, Katherine wished she'd told Althea she would meet her at the mall. But at the last moment someone pulled out of a slot less than a block away and she nabbed it before another driver took the opportunity.

Inside the main corridor of the courthouse, she hurried toward the annex where Althea's office was located. The last thing on her mind was running into Richard Marek. He was normally gone from the building at this time of day. Something out of the ordinary must have kept him in the office, she decided, as she spotted him striding straight toward her. Since the closest door to her opened into a janitor's closet, she could hardly dive through it. So she stood her ground and waited for him to approach her.

The tall, blond man was dressed impeccably in a gray suit and burgundy striped tie. His straight hair was smoothed perfectly to one side and though his features couldn't be classified as handsome, they would appear strong and appealing to most anyone who took the time to look at him. At the moment there was a wide smile on his face, yet Katherine didn't feel one speck of excitement at the sight of his greeting.

"Hello, Katherine. I didn't realize you were out and

about yet," he said warmly as he reached for her hand. "What are you doing here at the courthouse?"

She tried to smile back, but she knew the effort was lukewarm at best. "I'm meeting a friend for lunch." She pulled her hand from his grip while thinking his soft, manicured hand felt nothing like Lonnie's strong, rough palm and long fingers. "In fact, if you'll excuse me, Mr. Marek, I'm running a little late."

"How many times have I told you to call me Richard? And don't be so hasty to get away," he said pleasantly. "You haven't shown the baby to me yet."

Flustered, and trying her best not to show it, Katherine pulled the blanket back from David, while Richard moved closer. As he bent over the baby, she noticed he smelled like a forest of fir trees, instead of like the subtle scents of a man.

"Well, he looks like you, Katherine. You must be proud."

Katherine glanced furtively beyond his shoulder. Hopefully Althea would show up in a moment or two and save her. "Enormously."

"What did you name him?"

She looked at the tax assessor and thought how very opposite he was from the man she loved. "David. Lonnie David."

His brows puckered slightly. "Lonnie. Hmm. That's an...uncommon name. From your family?"

If Lonnie wanted to call his name redneck that was one thing, he had the right. But if Richard Marek tried it, she was going to put him in his place.

Lifting her chin, she said, "No. From a friend. A very close friend." Who wanted to be more, she thought silently. So what was she doing here? Why wasn't she back in Hereford, getting ready for Lonnie to come home from work? That was where she wanted to be. Where every particle in her body had ached to be for the past three weeks.

"So when are you planning on coming back to work? You really don't look as if you need your whole six weeks of maternity leave to recuperate. In fact, you look great."

She could feel her expression turning frosty, but she couldn't help it. He wasn't man enough to admit that his attitude was purely selfish. And suddenly she was thinking just how unselfish, how very giving and thoughtful, Lonnie had been to her. How could she have walked away from him when he'd been everything she'd ever dreamed about?

Because she'd been scared. So very scared of loving him and then losing him.

"My maternity leave isn't just about my physical health, Mr. Marek. It's also about the baby and the opportunity to spend time with him, bond with him. In case you didn't realize it, that's important to both of us."

His face reddened slightly, and he glanced at the people coming and going in the wide corridor. "Oh, I didn't mean it that way, Katherine. I—well, Rena just can't handle things in the office the way you do." Moving a step closer, he placed his hand on her arm and lowered his head toward hers to whisper, "I've missed you, Katherine. Really missed you. And now that you've had the baby, I think you and I need to have a long talk. It isn't good for the boy to be without a father."

Infuriated by his forward behavior, she snatched her

arm away from his grasp. "The 'boy' has a name. It's David. And now that you've brought this up, I'm happy that I've run into you like this, because you're right. We do need to have a talk. But as far as I'm concerned, the talk needs to be just long enough to tell you that you might as well keep Rena on permanently. I won't be coming back. Now if you'll excuse me, my friend is waiting."

His eyes bulged and his jaw dropped, but whatever he was going to say he could say to the wall, because Katherine hurriedly stepped around him and rushed down to the end of the corridor where Althea was waiting patiently.

"Hi, honey! Gee, you look beautiful. Except for that glower on your face." Her features puckered with a comical frown. "What did Marek say to you, anyway?"

Not daring to glance back, Katherine took Althea by the upper arm and urged her toward the nearest exit. "Come on. I'll tell you about it in the car."

Five minutes later Althea was zipping in and out of lunch hour traffic while Katherine tried to explain what had just taken place between her and the tax assessor.

"You told him you quit? Just like that?" Althea exclaimed as a driver suddenly stopped in front of her, forcing her to jam on the brakes.

Nodding stiffly, Katherine looked at her friend. "I realize it all sounds impulsive, Althea. But you should have heard the man! He had this assuming attitude that he and I…that we had a future together. And I've never encouraged him one whit! Why, he even had the gall to suggest that David needed a father. As if *I* didn't know that. And just as though *he* was the man for the job! I can't put up with it any longer, Althea. Good salary or not, I can't work under that sort of strain."

Althea darted her a concerned look. "What are you going to do?"

With a long sigh Katherine dropped her forehead into her hand. "Find another job. That's all I can do. David and I have to eat. We have to have a roof over our heads and what savings I have won't last long. Do you have any ideas?"

"Yeah, I have one great idea. Go back to that cowboy you've fallen in love with."

Katherine's head jerked up and she stared at Althea's profile as the woman continued to negotiate the busy traffic. "How do you——"

Swatting a hand through the air, Althea interrupted, "Oh, don't bother to deny it. Since you've come back home, he's all you've talked about. You're crazy about the man and you're miserable without him. What I can't figure is why you left him in the first place."

Katherine swallowed as the tears that were always nearby began to burn her eyes. "I guess I do love Lonnie," she quietly admitted. "But that doesn't necessarily mean I should have stayed out there."

Althea surprised her by chuckling. "Why? You don't love someone by running off from them."

Katherine drew in a ragged breath and let it out. "You do when you're scared, Althea. And I'm plenty scared. Over and over I keep picturing myself telling Lonnie how I feel—that I love him—and then later, after he's tired of me…well, he tells me it's over."

Whipping the economy car into the parking lot of a

fast-food restaurant, Althea left the motor and the heater running.

"Honey, I'm not an expert on romance. Tom and I have been together since high school. If I didn't have him I wouldn't know the first thing about finding a man to love or having him find me. But I can sure as heck see that there's no difference between losing your sheriff later and being here in Fort Worth and not having him in your life now." She reached for Katherine's hands and squeezed them with encouragement. "Katherine, you've had a lot to think about lately. This thing with your mother—"

Katherine released something between a sob and a laugh. "Oh God, Althea, don't call her my mother. She wasn't my mother. She lied to me all those years. And my father—the one who I thought ran out on her and me—he never existed. Everything I've ever believed in, my mother, my father, even Walt—they were all phonies. I don't know what or who to believe in anymore," she mumbled with anguish.

"You believed in Lonnie enough to name your child after him."

Katherine thought about that for long moments, and as she did she realized she'd believed in him from the very start. She'd fallen in love with him that night he drank that horrible instant coffee with her and ate vanilla wafers as though she'd served him a delicious slice of chocolate cake.

I'm a sucker for sweets. Especially two-crust pies. You ever make those, Miss Katherine?

Lonnie's simple words from that night suddenly came back to her again and, as they did, tears flowed

into her eyes. He wasn't suave, but he was straightfor-
ward and true. He was the only man she could ever love.
Seeing Richard and having him come on to her had
brought that fact home to her even more.

"You know, Althea, Lonnie's not had an easy life.
First his father was killed and then his mother snapped
and just ran off and left him with the neighbors. And
then there was a woman he thought he wanted to
marry—she walked out on him. But in spite of all of that
he wants to have a family. He wants David and me to
be his family. Where is his courage coming from? From
being a lawman?"

Althea gave her a knowing smile. "Love. It gives us
the courage to do things we'd otherwise never be capable of doing. You love Lonnie. That's all the courage
you need to go to him."

As Katherine considered her friend's advice, a heavy
weight began to lift from her shoulders. Hope tried to
flicker in her heart, but doubt quickly stepped in and she
bit worriedly on her lip as she looked at Althea.

"You're right. I have to find the courage to go to
him," Katherine told her. "But what if it's too late? I
walked away from him. He might not welcome me
back. He might think I'm no better than the woman who
dumped him before. And I couldn't blame him if he
did."

"You'll never know until you try," Althea gently
suggested. "But something tells me he'll be very glad
to see you."

A week passed before Katherine could complete
her packing, close out her lease on the apartment and
utilities, plus have her car tuned up for the seven- or

eight-hour trip to Hereford. Since she'd made her decision to go to Lonnie, she hadn't looked back, and today, as she pushed her little car westward into the vast Texas plains, she felt elated and fearful at the same time.

She'd not talked to Lonnie once since she'd driven his old Ford into town and caught the bus back to Fort Worth. Several times she'd asked herself why he hadn't attempted to call her, but each time she stopped herself from analyzing the question. She didn't want to think, even for a moment, that her leaving had killed all of Lonnie's feelings for her. She didn't want to believe that her own cowardice had ruined something so precious.

Thankfully the weather was clear and relatively mild for December in West Texas. She pushed the little car to drive the speed limit on the interstate and stopped only when David needed feeding or attending to. Even so, it was nearly dark when she entered Deaf Smith County, and she quickly made the decision to avoid Lonnie's office in Hereford. Barring an emergency somewhere in the county, he would more than likely be home now.

With that in mind, she turned her car onto the farm-to-market road that would take her to the Rafter C. And as she drove, she fervently prayed.

"Mitch, I told you not to be talking to Lester about me taking off a few days!" Lonnie barked into the telephone. "Why in tarnation did you disobey me?"

Unaffected by his boss's outburst, the young deputy said, "Because you needed to be disobeyed. If you're going to Fort Worth to see Katherine, someone needs to take over for you. Lester is next in line to you."

"Lester has his hands full already. His wife has been ill, and he's been having trouble with that disc in his back again. He needs time off himself."

"Guess that leaves me to fill in, then, doesn't it?" Mitch didn't hesitate to suggest.

In spite of himself, Lonnie had to smile. For some reason, Mitch reminded him of himself about ten years ago when he'd been a fresh young deputy raring to go.

"I don't know about that, Mitch. I'm not sure I want to leave the whole department in your hands. The bank could be completely cleaned out while you were down at the diner charming the waitresses."

"Oh, shoot, Lonnie—I mean, Sheriff—I wouldn't be doing any womanizing. At least, not while you were away. And—"

All of a sudden Lonnie caught the faint sound of a car driving toward the house. "Just a minute, Mitch. I think I hear someone outside. I'll call you back later."

Curious, Lonnie glanced out the windows at the beam of headlights sweeping the front yard. Who in heck would be coming to visit him at this hour? If this was about some damn stolen goat, he was going to send the caller packing, and quick.

Snatching up a denim jacket, he shrugged it on and stepped out into the pool of the porch light. As he did, he saw a woman emerging from the shadows. A woman with a baby in her arms.

His heart stopped, then began to pound like a drum. "Katherine! Is that you?"

She didn't answer until she reached the porch, and by then he could see clearly for himself that it was her, the very woman his heart had been aching for.

"Hello, Lonnie."

Stunned, he stepped slowly toward her and reached for the baby. "What…how did you get here?"

Katherine made a motion over her shoulder at the car parked near the yard fence. "I drove."

His eyes grew wide. "From Fort Worth? Alone?"

She nodded. "Yes. Just David and me. Were you expecting me to bring someone with me?"

He cuddled the baby into the crook of his left arm and as he did, he decided he'd never held a more precious bundle in his life. "I wasn't expecting you, period," he said.

As soon as his words were out, her head dropped with regret. "No," she mumbled quietly, "I don't expect you were."

Still stunned, his mind spinning at her unexpected appearance, Lonnie took her by the upper arm and led her toward the door. "Come on, it's cold out here, and you and the baby must be tired."

She looked up at him, her eyes both wary and hopeful. "You mean—I'm still welcome?"

He stared at her as joy, disbelief and hope all swept through him in one amazing rush. "Oh, Katherine! Did you honestly think you wouldn't be?"

Not waiting for an answer, he opened the door and ushered her inside the warm room. After he'd shut the door behind him, he carried David to the couch and placed him carefully on the cushion nearest the warmth of the fireplace.

Sinking down beside the baby, Lonnie momentarily ignored Katherine and pulled the blanket back for a better look at the boy. "Oh, he's grown since you've been gone! Really grown. But what's happened to all that dark hair he had? He looks like a plucked chicken."

Smiling nervously, she approached the couch and stood near Lonnie's knee. The urge to reach out and touch his shoulder was so great she had to make a fist at her side to stop herself.

"He lost most of it," she said huskily. "That was just baby hair. He'll get it back and more."

"Has he been well?"

His concern for David caused love to pour from her heart like an ever-flowing fountain. "The pediatrician says he's the picture of health."

"That's good. I've been wondering about him. Trying to imagine what he looked like now. He's going to make you a fine son, Katherine."

She drew in a deep, bracing breath as he pulled the blanket carefully up over the baby's shoulders. "I was hoping you'd say *our* son, Lonnie."

A pregnant silence lasted for what seemed like an eternity before he finally glanced up at her. When he did, the incredulous look on his face caused her throat to choke with emotion.

"*Our* son? Is that what you said?"

Smiling tearfully, she nodded and then she said in a choked, broken voice, "Oh, Lonnie. I've been...so stupid. Forgive me. Please, forgive me."

Instantly he was on his feet and dragging her into his arms. Burying his face in her hair, he said, "I don't know what's brought about this change. And right now it doesn't matter. Nothing matters except that you're here."

She flung her arms around his waist and clung to him

tightly as joy beat inside her like a wild bird soaring through a golden sky. "Oh Lonnie, I've been miserable without you. Absolutely miserable," she mumbled against his chest. "I don't want to live without you. Please tell me I don't have to."

These past weeks without Katherine and the baby, Lonnie had wondered if he would ever feel happiness again. Now it bubbled up in him like an effervescent drink, fizzing inside his head until he could hardly speak, much less think.

"As if I'd ever turn you away," he growled.

Bringing his hands beneath her jaw, he used his thumbs to tilt her face up to his.

Instantly Katherine went up on tiptoe to greet his lips with hers. The result was a deep, hungry kiss that left her moaning and clinging to his shoulders as her legs threatened to buckle beneath her.

Over and over he kissed her lips and then her cheeks, her forehead, her chin, until eventually his mouth moved back to her lips to hover there. "Will David be all right where he is?" he whispered.

The baby was sound asleep and warmed by the fire. Since he was still too young to roll, there wasn't any danger in letting him continue to sleep right where he lay.

Katherine nodded as her heart began to pound with anticipation. "He'll be fine."

Her answer was all that Lonnie was waiting for, and with one sweeping movement he scooped her up in his big arms and carried her out of the living room.

Down a short hall and then into his bedroom, he crossed the small space to the side of the bed and stood

Katherine on her feet. She shivered with longing as his hands raced up and down her body and his mouth founds hers again and again.

"I've dreamed of making love to you a thousand times," he murmured against her cheek. "But I never dreamed you'd come back to me—like this—on your own."

Her hands lifted to frame his dear, rugged face. "Oh, Lonnie, I left because I was afraid to love you."

His heart was pounding with the need to be inside her, to finally bond their bodies with the love that had already entwined their hearts.

"Oh, Katherine, I've been afraid, too. Afraid, since the very first day I met you. But everything is going to be all right now. If you love me—"

"If!" she exclaimed with disbelief. Then pressing kisses across his cheeks and onto his lips, she said, "I love you with every particle of my being. That's why I couldn't stay away. No matter what happens, I'll always love you."

Lonnie didn't need to hear more. His hands quickly found the bottom of her sweater and tugged it over her head. Next came her jeans, and his fingers fumbled nervously with the zipper before he finally managed to tug it down.

Katherine laughed softly as he struggled to pull the heavy denim down her legs, and for punishment Lonnie tossed her back onto the mattress and gave the jeans one hard yank that left both her and the bed bouncing.

Once the offending garment was tossed out of the way, he stripped down to his boxer shorts and quickly climbed onto the mattress with her. For the next few minutes his hands worshipped her soft, sleek body, and at the same time his mouth fed hungrily at hers.

In turn, Katherine eagerly explored the hardness of his arms and chest, the broadness of his shoulders and his lean, narrow waist. By the time her hands lowered to his muscled buttocks, he tore his mouth away from hers long enough to kick off his boxers and do away with her undergarments.

Once the lacy things were out of the way, his hands busied themselves by cupping her breasts and kneading their fullness. When his head dropped and his tongue began to lave her nipples, Katherine began to ache in a way she'd never ached before and she thrust her hips toward his in a silent plea.

"Maybe this is a little late," he said between gulps of air, "but are you okay now—to do this?"

"Yes," she whispered. "I've already had a checkup. But I haven't been on birth control pills long enough to eliminate any chance of getting pregnant."

His eyes warm and gentle, he searched her face. "Would it bother you to get pregnant again? With my child?"

Her hands skimmed over his back. "No. In fact, I would love it."

Wonder filled his face and lifted the corners of his lips in a smile of disbelief. "But you've just now gotten over David's birth."

With a seductive chuckle, she aligned her hips with his. "And I'll have nine months to get ready for the next one. Unless you take me for a drive in another ice storm. Then I might just have eight and a half months."

His eyes glinted with anticipation. "Katherine, you

naughty girl. I can see it's going to take a sheriff like me to keep you in line."

Sighing with sheer happiness, she pulled his head down to hers. "That's just what I've been thinking," she murmured against his lips.

Words between them were suddenly forgotten as once again Lonnie began to kiss her, to fill her with unbearable heat. In a matter of moments, she opened her legs and guided him inside. Lonnie's low growl of pleasure flooded the room and was instantly followed by Katherine's guttural moan as the two of them began to move together in perfect rhythm, bound by a love that neither could deny.

A long time later, Katherine lay in the warm crook of Lonnie's arm. Near the bed, less than an arm's length away, David slept in a bassinet that Katherine had brought with her from Fort Worth.

As she drew lazy circles with her forefinger across Lonnie's chest, she said, "This morning I was miserable. I was terrified that I had ruined any chance for us to be together. Now, a few hours later, I'm the happiest woman alive." Tilting her head up, she placed a kiss on his jaw. "I don't deserve someone as understanding as you."

"Hmm. I know you don't," he teased. "But I'll squeeze some sort of payment out of you over the next—oh, I'd say fifty or sixty years."

Smiling, she snuggled her face against his shoulder. "Fifty or sixty years, huh? That sounds like a marriage deal to me."

"I wouldn't want any other sort of deal." Propping his head up on one hand, he used the other one to gently stroke her cheek. "So are you going to marry me, Katherine McBride?"

"Are you sure you want to marry me now, since I've joined the ranks of the unemployed?"

His brows rose with interest. "Too much has been going on since you got here. I hadn't thought about your job. What happened?"

"I quit."

"And the tax man? You didn't mind telling him goodbye?"

She snuggled the front of her body close to his. "I saw him a few days ago at the courthouse. While he was talking, all I was thinking about was you. Just looking at him made me realize I could never love any man but you."

"If that's the case, then I'm glad you saw him." His arm circled her waist and squashed her naked body possessively against his. "And as far as you being unemployed, I'm not really worried that your marrying me for my money. Especially when I don't have any to speak of. Now, you, on the other hand, should be a little concerned about my motives."

Her brows arched upward. "Really? Why should I be concerned?"

His hand slid from her shoulder to her hip and back again. "Because you're a Ketchum heir. You have a moral, if not legal, right to a part of their fortune. And I'm more than sure they're going to be glad to share it with you. If you'll let them."

Her head was suddenly reeling with the implication of Lonnie's suggestion. All her life she'd lived modestly. She'd never dreamed of having more. And now, entwined in Lonnie's warm embrace, she realized that money was only an afterthought. All she'd ever really need was him, and their children.

"The past few weeks have given me plenty of time to think, Lonnie. And believe me, I've done a lot of it. Mostly about you. But the Ketchums, too. Those letters you left on the coffee table for me—I read them. And afterward I knew I couldn't continue to live in denial about my family. Amelia Ketchum and Noah Rider were my parents. Celia was just trying to help her sister by raising me. And Noah—he didn't desert me. He died because he was going to tell everyone that I was his daughter."

He sighed with relief. "I'm glad you can finally admit that. But I think you need to take it one step further and meet your family."

Tilting her head back, she studied his face. "As long as you'll be with me."

With a happy grunt, he rolled them both over until he was flat on his back and Katherine was sprawled on top of him.

"Always, my little darling. Always."

Epilogue

Christmas Eve had finally arrived on the T Bar K, and the big ranch house was elaborately decorated for the occasion. Trimmed trees, hanging tinsel and poinsettias of every shade adorned the many rooms. Scented candles burned and vied with the delicious scents of baked desserts and roasted meat coming from the kitchen. In the formal dining room, two long tables were elegantly set for the guests who were soon to arrive. Champagne was chilling, and a pianist, along with a violinist, had been hired to provide Gershwin and Cole Porter love tunes.

However, none of those things was the real reason the ranch was in such a festive mood. A wedding was about to take place, and the Ketchums couldn't have been happier to see their new sibling marrying an old friend.

"I can truly say that I've never seen a more beautiful

bride," Victoria said as she stood back and eyed Katherine.

Up until now, the bedroom Katherine had chosen to use as a dressing room had been chaos, as women had rushed in and out and everyone had clustered around to help with her hair and makeup. But as the time grew near for the ceremony to start, the two sisters were finally alone.

Blushing at the compliment, Katherine glanced down at the long, ivory-colored dress she was wearing. It was made of heavy satin and the décolletage was just low enough to make her feel sexy and elegant at the same time. Her hair was piled in curls atop her head, and hanging from her ears were pearl and diamond earrings. A special gift from Lonnie.

"I'm sure you looked far more beautiful when you married Jess," she told her sister.

Victoria laughed. "Not hardly. Jess and I had a quick wedding in the judge's chambers. I wore a special dress, but nothing like what you have on."

"I'm sure you were beautiful anyway," Katherine insisted. "And from seeing the two of you together, I'm fairly certain you're just as married as Lonnie and I will be."

Patting her very pregnant tummy, Victoria grinned. "I think it's safe to say we're stuck for life."

Katherine went over to her newfound sister and gently touched her shoulder. "Are you feeling all right, Victoria? No back twinges or anything? You're due date is just two weeks away now. Labor could begin anytime," she said, then, suddenly catching herself, she laughed. "I guess I *am* nervous. I'm forgetting you're the doctor here. You know all about that sort of thing."

Smiling, Victoria shook her head. "Don't worry about me. I'm fine. I'm not even tired. I'm going to dance all evening. If I can keep Jess on his feet," she added jokingly.

Katherine sighed as she looked at the other woman. When she'd first met Victoria a few days ago, she'd felt as though she was looking in a mirror. But since then she'd learned that she and her sister had much more in common than their looks. And to say they'd hit it off would be quite an understatement. Katherine had never felt so loved or wanted in her life.

"Well, I feel a little guilty about having this big wedding," Katherine admitted. "Lonnie and I didn't need it. You and your family have gone to way too much expense for us."

"Nonsense," Victoria countered. "We love any excuse to have a celebration. And it's a small amount to pay to say welcome to the family."

Katherine's eyes were suddenly misty. "I can't understand you and your brothers, Victoria. You've been so wonderful to me. Another family might not have thought of me as a welcome addition."

Victoria's hands came up to clasp Katherine's shoulders. "Listen, Katherine, our father, Tucker, is somewhat of a legend around here, and we loved him. But now that we are grown, we can look back and see that he wasn't the perfect husband for our mother. She must have been desperately hungry for affection and she obviously found it with Noah. We're glad that she experienced that little bit of happiness with him. Because you see, we loved her, too. I just wish that you could have grown up here with us—where you belonged."

Choked with emotion, Katherine whispered, "So do I."

With a last pat for Katherine's shoulder, Victoria turned and crossed the room to where a small box lay on a dresser. Picking it up, she opened the lid and pulled out a single strand of pearls.

Carrying the necklace back to Katherine, she said, "These belonged to our mother. I know she would be very, very happy if she could see you wearing them now."

Too gripped with emotion to speak, she allowed Victoria to hook the pearls around her neck and then the two sisters left the quietness of the bedroom.

Ross, who was going to give Katherine away, was standing in the hallway, just outside of the living room, waiting to take her by the arm. As he did, the wedding march began to play and the two of them moved forward.

Katherine felt as though she were walking on clouds as she entered the room that was crammed full of family and friends. For a second, her gaze skittered over the crowd and she caught sight of Marina, the Ketchums' long-time housekeeper, holding little David and next to her, Bella, Ross's wife, was dabbing her eyes with a handkerchief. Then Katherine's attention zeroed in on the front of the room, where, beneath an arch of white poinsettias and flanked by tall, flickering candles, Lonnie stood waiting to make her his wife.

Next to him, Seth was standing as his best man, and to the right side of them, the minister waited with his Bible in hand. Just behind the men, past the big picture window that looked down upon the ranch yard, Katherine could see the twinkling lights the cowboys had

strung along the eaves of the bunkhouse. Higher up, beyond the mountain peaks, the night sky was adorned
with its own Christmas stars. And for a moment, as
Katherine caught a glimpse of them, she hoped her parents could see what the two of them had given her.

* * * * *

From

SPECIAL EDITION™

The next romance from Marie Ferrarella's miniseries

Born to heal, destined to fall in love!

Available December 2004.

THE M.D.'S SURPRISE FAMILY
SE #1653
by Marie Ferrarella

Raven Songbird came to neurosurgeon Peter Sullivan for a
consultation—and before she knew it, Raven fell in love with
the reclusive doctor. Would this free spirit convince him
that they were destined for happiness?

Available at your favorite retail outlet.

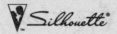

Coming in December 2004 from

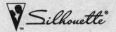

SPECIAL EDITION™

and award-winning author

Laurie Paige

The latest book in her exciting miniseries.

Seven cousins—bound by blood, honor and tradition—bring a whole new meaning to "family reunion!"

A KISS IN THE MOONLIGHT

(SE #1654)

Lyric Gibson had fallen hard for handsome Trevor Dalton a year ago, but a misunderstanding drove them apart. Now she and her aunt have been invited to visit the Dalton ranch in Idaho, and Lyric is elated. The attraction between them is as strong as ever, even with their rocky history. Lyric is determined to win back Trevor's trust—and his heart—at any cost!

Don't miss this emotional story—only from Silhouette Books!

Available at your favorite retail outlet.

Coming in December from

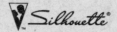

SPECIAL EDITION™

and beloved author

Allison Leigh

THE TRUTH ABOUT THE TYCOON

(SE #1651)

Desperate to see justice served, CEO
Dane Rutherford took matters into his own
hands and headed to Montana to track down
the man who kidnapped his sister. But his
mission got seriously sidetracked when he
literally collided with Hadley Golightly. And it
wasn't long before this tempting brunette was
showing this alpha male that sometimes the
best things in life are the ones you can't control!

Don't miss this captivating new book!

Available at your favorite retail outlet.